AR

"Bad things do happen to good boys. And, sometimes, Logan Michaels finds out, they get much, much worse. A coming-of-age tale of the human spirit, redemption and a son's love."

—MARY R. ARNO, author of *Thanksgiving*

"I became invested with his characters early on and I cared about what happened to them. I have come to realize, through my own writing, that we are all trying to provide a snapshot of a place in time. Mr. Roberts does exactly that. I'd read more from him."

—WILLIAM LOBB, author of *The Third Step*

"Roberts has written about the roller-coaster life of Logan Michael, beginning at the apex and then hurtling down through bad decisions and hard luck. His teenage hubris leads to drugs and drink instead of college and success. But the roller-coaster then promises a thrilling upturn when he confronts his mother's mortality. No doubt a sequel is in Roberts' plans."

—BRUCE JOEL BRITTAIN, author of *Brother Daniel's Good News Revival*

The Crossroads of
Logan Michaels

by James M. Roberts

© Copyright 2018 James M. Roberts

ISBN 978-1-63393-648-5

Published by

 köehlerbooks™

210 60th Street
Virginia Beach, VA 23451
800–435–4811
www.koehlerbooks.com

THE CROSS ROADS

OF LOGAN MICHAELS

JAMES M. ROBERTS

VIRGINIA BEACH
CAPE CHARLES

For my loving family.

Author's Note

This is a work of fiction. While many of the events are drawn from personal experiences or observations, the characters and their actions and dialogue are imagined.

CHAPTER 1

AGE OF INNOCENCE

eing in a new town, and leaving all of my old friends, scared me. I knew I was good at baseball and basketball, but I worried whether I would still be good in North Andover. Summer was ending, but I couldn't complain. We'd had fun times camping in Maine, while my little brother, Jared, and I got into mischief. My friends from Andover called me and said we should still hang out, even though we would be in different towns.

The summer came to an end and I was ready for third grade at my new school. Monday arrived and I looked out the window at the playground and saw all the kids. Living across the street from the school wasn't all that bad. I grabbed my bag and kissed my mother and high-fived my dad before walking over to the school yard. There was a steep hill I slowly ran down, and then I ran across a field of kids kicking a soccer ball. I aimlessly walked around, checking out the playground, kicking my feet, and watching the kids play before the bell rang. Our house was so close that I could see my mom staring through the window at me.

The bell rang as I watched kids line up. We "pledged allegiance" outside and then walked to class. *Being the new kid sucks,* I thought, as I sat down next beside a boy named Grant.

"What's your name, kid?"

"Logan," I said.

"Got a last name?"

"Michaels. My name is Logan Michaels."

"You play any sports?"

"Yeah, baseball and basketball," I replied.

"You any good?"

I laughed and said, "Let's play at recess and find out."

Recess arrived; we grabbed the basketball immediately and ran over to the hoops. After a couple of shots, the fifth-graders came over and tried to kick us off the court. Grant and I were not giving up that easily, though, and we said, "Let's play for it."

They laughed as they confidently threw the ball to me. I caught it and shot. *SWISH!!* The game started out with two people watching, and by the end of recess, Grant and I had the whole recess crowd around us cheering. "ICE! ICE! ICE!" the older kids yelled. My last shot was in the air as everyone was watching: game point and *SWISH!*

We won by one point, and that day established my new nickname, *Ice,* because I had taken about twenty shots and had missed only two. The older kids said that we could play with them anytime, and I became popular on my first day. I ran home right after school, ready to tell my mom everything.

I walked in the house and saw Jared playing in the kitchen while my mom prepared dinner. The fall air was warm and crisp, with a sourdough bread smell lingering. I threw my bag down and told my mother about my day. She smiled and looked content as she continued to cook dinner. My mother would always smile when she saw me and Jared. We would hang out until dinnertime, and wait for Dad to come home. We would play video games, run around the house, and play in the yard; we always had so much energy.

My dad would come home, kick off his work boots, kiss my mom, and roughhouse with us. We typically tackled him as soon as he came through the door. Jared and I would lose to Dad, of course; he seemed like the strongest guy in the world. After dinner, we would rush outside to play basketball with our small hoop in the yard until it got dark. My mom would yell out the window about how we needed to do our homework, and we would come inside once the sun set.

Realizing that I might have a career in basketball, I had Dad sign me up for the North Andover booster club team. We walked into tryouts; he was definitely the youngest father in there, being only twenty-eight years old. Most dads were in their late thirties. As tryouts began, he introduced himself to the fathers. Everyone made the team, but I guess the tryouts were to see how they could split up the kids to make fair teams.

After waiting a week for the results, I finally received a call from Mr. Stone, the coach of the Hawks. He welcomed me onto the team, told me the practice schedule, and said, "See you there, Logan." I hopped off the phone and ran into my parents' room to tell them the good news. I jumped on the bed and then noticed something strange: my mother was crying and my father was rubbing her back with a worried look on his face.

"What's wrong?" I asked. My mom hugged me. My brother walked in quietly, looking unsettled as he hugged my mom and dad.

"It's my mom, Nana," she said. "She's been diagnosed with Alzheimer's and is very sick."

"What's Alzheimer's?" I asked.

"It makes you forget who you are, Logan." I was confused, but just hugged my mother back as she wiped her tears.

We had been a tight-knit family before moving. My mom and

dad grew up on the same street and met when they were children. My grandparents on both sides were always coming over to visit us, and we would go to their houses. We even went to church with them on Sundays. Jared and I called my mother's parents "Nana" and "Papa;" we called my father's parents "Granpy" and "Grammy." I was closest to Nana.

Sitting in my room that night, I didn't know whether I should be excited for basketball season, or sad for my Nana. It made me understand that pleasure and pain always went hand in hand. *One minute you're up, and the next, you're down*, I thought as I shut my eyes.

We all visited my Nana that weekend, and I just couldn't look at her the same way I had before. She was no different, but when I saw her, all I could think about was the Alzheimer's and about whether she would one day forget me. It made me sad to see her like this, and to then look over at Papa and see him in the rocking chair shaking his knees; it was nice to see that he was smiling. He would always talk so loudly; I guess he had trouble hearing, but was never afraid to say what was on his mind.

Several cousins and their parents were visiting Nana and Papa. There were so many kids of similar ages on my mom's side of the family. My mother had two brothers and a sister, and between them they had six kids, all roughly my age. We would spend the holidays together and go camping on the Cape and have a blast playing sports.

I was the closest with my cousin Tim. We would sleep over at each other's house all of the time, and would often get in trouble together. We would talk about being confused when we found out that Nana was diagnosed with Alzheimer's, but agreed that we couldn't tell any difference in her behavior.

It was always a bit scary visiting my father's side of the family. Some days, we would go over there after visiting Nana's and Papa's house. Dad's parents' house was old and scary, but must have had a million rooms. It had an old bar with tools and old rusty cars, which was kind of creepy. There was a large pit underneath the garage and I always wondered what the heck was down there, but was too afraid to go see.

My dad had three sisters and a brother, and they had seven kids between them. I was closest to Ryan, but he wasn't really into sports like my cousin Tim and me. Ryan was more occupied with playing in the garage with tools, making traps, and playing in the woods. The one thing that really got my blood pumping was the rope swing the two of us had made.

It was attached to a tree above the garage, directly over a pit. We would swing over the pit, twenty feet in the air; it was such a rush. My brother Jared always wanted to try, but I would never let him. I tended to be kind of hard on him because he wanted to be right next to me all of the time.

○ ○ ○

Basketball season was starting and, after my first practice, I was selected to start on our team. I loved the attention. I was the only kid on the team who wanted his parents to show up for the games. The reason was simple: my mom was beautiful and young, and my dad was tough-looking and muscular and looked like a kid. I wanted to show them off.

The season was great, and I was one of the best players in the league. The kids at school would talk to me about the games and about how good I was; it felt amazing to have people counting on me each game. The girls noticed me even though I was barely ten years old but I was very shy when it came to the opposite sex.

Katrina was her name—my first crush. She had beautiful, long, straight blonde hair and a killer smile. In class, I would stare at her out of the corner of my eye. Once I noticed her, I promised myself that I would talk with her someday. I just had to work up the courage. *Guess again!* Third grade and fourth grade passed and still not a single word!

Was it possible that the girl of my dreams would get away? I couldn't believe that two years had gone by, and I still hadn't even spoken to Katrina.

How was it that my basketball team won the championship two years in a row, I started as the pitcher for the Little League's National League Rockies, got straight A's in school, and had tons of friends, but still could not talk to a girl? Hard to believe that even with so much success, I still couldn't do it. *I will work the courage up one day*, I thought. After all, I was only eleven.

Although school was great, things at home were getting kind of shaky. My mother and father would fight almost every night; Jared and I would listen from outside of their door some nights. A lot of what I heard concerned money and problems with elders. Mainly, things were tough with my Nana, and she could hardly remember who anyone was anymore. It was hard to see my mother, beautiful like an angel, and imagine that one day she might not be able to recognize her little boy when she looked into his eyes. It made me sad. *No one deserves this*, I thought.

North Andover was treating me great, however. I had two best friends who lived up the street, cousins named John and Jason. There must have been twenty kids that lived on my street. John and Jason came from wealthy families. Their parents were much older than mine, and they had big houses with swimming pools and huge yards with manicured lawns. I loved staying over at their houses, and dreamed that one day I could have a house like that. They were my first real friends when I came to North Andover; we would play sports together, go to the beach, and do other normal kid things.

The best nights I can remember were when we would get the whole neighborhood of kids together and play "Manhunt," a game when one team of kids would hide throughout the neighborhood while the other team would try to find them. Jared would play sometimes, but I didn't want him to get lost in the neighborhood. Jared was much younger than me, which made it hard on him. I was going to be twelve years old, and he was only eight. Don't get me wrong, I think we were probably two of the closest brothers anyone could imagine, but when it came to me hanging out with my friends, I treated him cruelly and often told him that he couldn't play.

Jared would often get hurt playing with my friends and me. However, whether he was hurt from smacking his head, falling off his bike, or scraping his knees, he always managed to continue playing. The day that still haunts me is July 9th during the summer before middle school.

Jared and I were playing in the backyard beside a small crabapple tree that produced small apples we picked to throw at cars in the street. I know it wasn't the best idea, especially since we lived on a street that was busy. We would both look around the house and wait for a car to come flying down the street. As it approached, *BAM!* We would throw the apples and then run into the house. We got caught one time and, trust me, Dad screamed at us until I never wanted to look at that tree again. That incident stopped us for a couple of weeks; instead, we would throw water balloons at the local paper boy when he walked by. After getting bored with that, though, we returned to that old leaning crabapple tree.

SMACK! We laughed and watched the car speed up the street, confused. We both ran around the house as quickly as possible. I made it in the house first and shut the screen door behind me, locking Jared out.

Our door was old, lightweight, and made of glass; Jared banged on it and yelled at me as I laughed. He continued to knock on the door like he was being chased. *Bang! Bang! Bang!* He hit the door harder and harder as I laughed on the other side. My mom was ignoring our antics from the other room. Again, *Bang! Bang!* Then *SMASH!* As the door shattered and glass flew everywhere and into my face, I ducked to cover myself. Jared screamed.

Looking up, I instantly panicked; I had never seen so much blood in my life. Blood was rushing down Jared's arm, and it looked like he had dumped a bucket of paint over his wrist. He cried and I started to scream and cry even more than he did. My mom sprinted down the hall and grabbed Jared. She covered his wrist while I apologized, crying hysterically; I felt so guilty for what I had done. *This is all my fault*, I thought.

Mom sped to Lawrence General Hospital while holding a crying Jared, his whole arm covered in blood. Mom remained calm during the ride and got us into the hospital. The doctor immediately grabbed Jared and took him into the emergency room. I was so sad to see him on the stretcher, screaming. *What the hell have I done*, I thought, as I continued to pace while my tears dripped onto the floor. Jared's screams were so loud that the whole waiting room could hear this poor eight year old boy for a half-hour straight. As I was pacing, I realized I had a sharp pain in my back, so I reached back under my shirt. I had been so worried about Jared, I didn't even care, until I pulled a two-inch-long piece of glass out of my back.

I needed Jared to be okay. I didn't need stitches, just a big bandage, and after a couple of hours, Jared emerged with five stitches. He had cut his wrist and the doctor said he had missed his tendons by a centimeter—if glass had hit them, he possibly might have never used his wrist again. Everyone was silent on the ride home. I think that we had all had enough for a while, and just wanted to let Jared get some rest. It was hard for me to look at myself, knowing that I had caused my brother's pain, but life went on.

For the rest of the summer, Jared and I took it easy. His arm took a couple of months to heal, and he was soon back to normal. I mainly practiced basketball at the school across the street every day to take my mind off things. My dad and I would play baseball across the street, too, since, after all, I was going into middle school in a month and would need to try out for the travel team. I needed to step up my game.

My brother got into hockey, and he would rollerblade and play with a couple of his friends at the school after his wrist healed. He was getting big for his age that summer, and had a killer slap shot. My dad signed him up to start playing so that we could both keep busy.

By the time middle school started, I was excited to play basketball—after all, I was *Ice.* I knew most of the eighth graders and, as for the ones I didn't know, I wanted to impress them with my game on the court. Tryouts came soon, and I immediately impressed my coaches and got drafted to play on the Merrimack Valley starting travel team as a starting shooting guard. Jared was playing defense on his hockey team; things were back to normal and going well.

My best friends, Jason and John, were not in my classes, though; they were a little more "advanced" than me in most subjects. It didn't really bother me; I mean, I was on the starting basketball team. I met a lot of different kids on my team and I liked them a lot. So Jason, John, and I started to separate a little bit, but we always managed to walk home together after school, since we lived right down the street, after all.

Middle school was my chance to shine. I was going to show the school how good I was at basketball this year. The first couple of games we played were so awesome; I loved traveling to different towns on the school bus. The feeling of butterflies, and feeling like my heart was in my throat, was a rush every game.

I quickly passed the ball to Tim and cut to the hoop; *a back door by Michaels, yes! Dribble, crossover, behind the back, jump shot, swish!* "Player of the Game goes to Logan Michaels."

The feeling was almost unimaginable. My parents would proudly watch their son score twenty points a game, quickly making a name for himself. Jared would also watch from the crowd, although he usually seemed bored: he wasn't really into basketball. He was more focused on hockey, at which he was amazing: when he put on his skates and padding, he was almost as tall as my dad. He had grown overnight, it seemed. He was by far the biggest kid on the ice. He outskated, outshot, and outplayed everyone. I'm not sure where our athleticism came from; I knew my dad had played recreational sports and so had my mom, but Jared and I were all-stars.

It was amazing to watch Jared shoot such a powerful slap shot. The wrist he had injured was stronger than ever, and he had the scar across it that always reminded me of that day. Jared's hockey games were usually on Sundays, which I loved. The leaves were falling, it was slightly cold, and the smell of my mom's hot chocolate made me feel so warm inside. We would all hop in Dad's beat-up car and drive over to the hockey rink to watch Jared play. I would scream in the stands for Jared as he skated speedily down the ice. "Take the shot, Jared!" *Shoot!*

◎ ◎ ◎

Sixth grade in middle school was so different from elementary. One difference was that the girls were so much more mature and developed. My locker was in the corner of the hallway, right next to the locker of this amazing girl. I would look over shyly, but she wouldn't see me. I was always hoping that one day she would glance back. I thought that maybe if I could become a huge basketball star, then she would give me some attention.

We had an old brown garage in our dirt driveway; it seemed like it was going to fall down at any point, but it never did. My dad had built a basketball hoop. The backboard was plywood and he screwed on an old rim. He attached it to this old garage, and it was exactly ten feet tall. Now, I could play every day throughout the year to win over my eighth-grade dream girl.

Jason and John and some neighborhood kids would come over and we would have awesome games every night. I would play until Mom called me in for supper.

The driveway was about twenty feet long and covered with big stones, and if the ball hit a stone, it would go flying. This helped me learn how to dribble. After dinner, I would go outside to play and shoot by myself. I would take fifty free throws a night until I hardly ever missed.

The sun would go down and I would come in to do homework as my mom and dad were in the other room, yelling and arguing. This seemed to happen more often these days. Mom would never let me see her sad, though. Jared would play video games and do his homework. The typical American family, I guess you could call it.

My basketball team was headed to our biggest game of the season, against Methuen. I had been practicing in that dirt driveway for weeks until the sun went down. When we were on the school bus driving to Methuen, I was quiet; my teammates were surprised that I was so focused and ready to go. Tipoff began, and I ran down the court to the three spot; Kevin passed the ball, my hands were steady and ready.

Jump fake, behind the back, under the legs to the hoop, taking the shot! Swish and a foul. I got to the foul line, and all I could imagine was being in my dirt driveway as I easily nailed the bonus shot. I ran back with a big smile on my face, excited that my hard work was paying off. The first half of the game ended and we were up by fifteen points; I alone had fifteen points and was four-for-four from the foul line. The second half started and I couldn't miss. I looked at my parents in the crowd and saw that they had just realized how amazing their son was at basketball.

All the parents were cheering, yelling for me, and I felt so high that day; it was amazing. My dream girl was going to love me.

The game ended and we won by a landslide. I finished the game with twenty-eight points and was eight-for-eight from the free-throw line. The game ball went to me and I rode home on the bus like I was king; things were going to change for me. The next day in school was fantastic—I got high-fives left and right as I walked down the hallway, and girls said hi to me as they smiled. I got to my locker and looked over at my tall, blonde, big-breasted, full-mouthed dream girl. She wasn't looking, and I anxiously began to walk over to introduce myself. I turned and faced her with my first step, but before I could, a guy ran over to her and kissed her. *Fuck!* I thought, as I slammed my locker shut and went to class. *What does he have that I don't?* I had attention from everyone except from the one person who mattered.

On the positive side, basketball made me quite popular and, as Jason and John focused more on classes, I was hanging with the cool kids, mainly the athletes. The school year went fine: I maintained B's and A's, had an amazing basketball season, and was looking forward to summer basketball leagues and my baseball season—maybe Katie, my heartthrob, would notice me then.

I tried out for the middle school baseball team a few months after basketball season. I made the team as a starting pitcher. The coach said that I had uncanny accuracy and that he was excited to see what I could do. Most of the kids from basketball were on the baseball team with me, so I began to grow close to them and drifted farther from Jason and John. Sadly, middle school divides people; my old friends were more studious and nerdy, whereas I was popular and great at sports.

Baseball was so different from Little League; the mounds were so much farther apart and the fields were huge. In the first game of the season, I was starting for the travel team, pitching. *STRIKE!* First pitch. Second pitch, *STRIKE!*

One more, Logan, let's do this, I said to myself. *STRIKE THREE! Three pitches and three strikes, where did I get this talent from?* Three batters up during my first inning and all strikeouts. My team cheered and won that game; no runs scored and I had ten strikeouts. Player of the Game went to me, and again my head was inflated with confidence.

School arrived, and Katie was at her locker; I couldn't stop staring. She was even more beautiful. Still nothing. No look, smile, or gesture. That night when I got home, I went to work at our old computer that my grandfather had given us. We had dial-up Internet and I created a screen for AOL; one of my basketball buddies had told me about it. I created a screen name and could instant-message friends in real time. *LMichaelsx75* was my screen name, and I linked up with my buddy Kevin. I then asked if he knew Katie's screen name, waiting anxiously for his reply. He laughed, sending "LOL," and then said, "Dude, just talk to her." I acted like it wasn't a big deal while anxiously waiting to see if he knew the name. *Kshellz* popped up, and my heart soared.

Thanks dude, see you tomorrow, I replied to Kevin. I opened my message box with the cursor just blinking and my chest tightened as I got up from my chair and paced back and forth. My mom called for dinner and I yelled back, "Give me a minute." I sat in the chair, and sent Katie a message. Then I ran downstairs to dinner; I didn't even want to see if she had responded. During dinner, I could barely eat a bite, and, immediately afterward I rushed up to the computer.

```
LMichaelsx75: Hey
```

No response, and it had been thirty minutes. *Shit! Why did I message her?* I got up to go downstairs when I heard a message notification sound.

Kshellz: Hi who's this?

LMichaelsx75: Logan

Kshellz: Do we know each other?

LMichaelsx75: Lol I don't think so, my locker is right next to yours

Kshellz: Lol hmm I'm not sure I know who you are, but Hi

LMichaelsx75: I'm in sixth grade, I play for the basketball and baseball team

Kshellz: Oh cool. Well come say hi to me tomorrow

LMichaelsx75: ok cool. Well nice meeting you. Bye

Kshellz: Night

Holy shit! It was happening: the girl of my dreams wanted me to talk with her. *But wait, she hasn't even seen me. What if she doesn't like me?* I rushed to my closest and began picking through all of my clothes; I needed to wear my coolest shirt. I picked out an Abercrombie shirt that I loved, and my favorite jeans and basketball shoes. I anxiously hopped into bed and dreamed about her naked body. I had watched a porno before, and was wondering if she looked anything like the girls in that film. My night was so long; it felt as if morning would never come.

I walked nervously into school the next morning. My hands were sweaty; my stomach was rumbling because I had missed breakfast, and my knees felt like they would collapse at any moment. My pitching arm felt like jelly. I turned the corner to the hallway where my locker was located, and there she was. She looked so pretty, even prettier than usual. *Was this for me?*

I wondered. I popped a couple pieces of gum into my mouth before walking over to her slowly.

"Katie? Hey, I'm Logan."

She smiled and said, "Hi!" Her smile made my body warm and tense. I walked her to her class down the hallway and we barely said a word. We awkwardly said goodbye to each other as the bell rang. The walk was probably only one minute long, but it had felt like an hour. After she walked into class, my body felt light again. I was so relieved; a weight had been lifted off of my shoulders. *OMG!* I walked to class feeling invulnerable and overwhelmed.

That whole day, I sat in classes thinking about her, the way her lips might taste, the way her breasts had looked. The day was a blur and ended quickly. That night, I messaged her again and we chatted about school and sports. I wanted to ask her to the dance coming up in a month, but I knew she had a boyfriend.

Weeks passed, and I hadn't talked to Katie again. It was just so stressful being near her; she made me nervous and I didn't want to ruin the one time we had talked. I focused on my baseball team and school; we were 3-0 and I was the number-one pitcher on the team. I won two games in a row and hadn't given up a run. Still, all I could think about was Katie and the big dance coming up. All of my friends on the team had dates, but I wanted to ask Katie. That night, I finally got the courage to message her again.

```
LMichaelsx75: Hey Katie

Kshellz: Hi!

LMichaelsx75: how are you?

Kshellz: I'm good thx. How are you?

LMichaelsx75: I'm good, tired from baseball
```

```
Kshellz: aww

LMichaelsx75: I have a question for you

Kshellz: yes?

LMichaelsx75: Are you going to the dance?

Kshellz: Yes of course

LMichaelsx75: Do you have a date?

Kshellz: Lol, ya my boyfriend

LMichaelsx75: Lol oh ya cool

Kshellz: what about you?

LMichaelsx75: Ya I have a date

Kshellz: awesome!

LMichaelsx75: save me a dance lol

Kshellz: Sure!
```

That night, I realized that Katie and I were just friends. *I need to find a way to make her mine,* I thought. Also, I didn't have a date, so I needed to find one quickly; if I showed up alone then Katie would know that I was a liar. There was this one girl I thought was kind of cute—Lauren. I messaged her immediately after signing off with Katie. She knew me, even though we didn't talk a lot, and she didn't have a date either.

I am such a wimp, messaging a girl that I hardly ever talk to and asking her to the dance, I thought. However, Lauren said "yes" right away, and we planned on meeting at her friend's house. A couple of my baseball and basketball friends were going with Lauren's friends, so at least we could all go together. I went to bed that night, had a date for the dance, but it was not a date with my dream girl. *Maybe one day I will get to dance with Katie.*

My mom helped me pick out a suit for the dance. She scrapped together the rest of the money that she had made from Mary Kay and bought me a beautiful suit. It seemed that no matter the circumstances, my mother would always support her family, have dinner ready, and treat my dad well. After we picked out my suit, we visited Nana and Papa.

Nana was getting really bad; she didn't even know her own daughter and grandson anymore. My uncle told us that she was going into a nursing home because it was hard for her to be on her own; she needed help. I saw my mother's childlike eyes water and I hugged her. I could never imagine this happening to my mom one day; it made me sad to see Mom suffering.

Papa looked depressed, rocking in his chair as he grunted, wearing the same green sweatshirt that he always wore. He never gave up on his wife, Eva, though; he was with her every day, even sitting in the chair next to her when she went to the nursing home. Their love seemed like an unspoken bond, and even though Eva couldn't really remember who he was anymore, when I saw them look into each other's eyes, I think that maybe she kind of did.

Again that night, my mother and father fought over money. He worked so hard and so did she, but neither had a "career." All of my friend's parents had a big house with nice cars, and it made me jealous at times. I almost felt like I wasn't worthy of being their friend because I didn't have a big house.

The day of the dance arrived, and my dad tied my tie for me and said, "Good luck." My mother kissed me and smiled, asking for pictures, and Jared laughed at me as I walked away nervously in my suit.

We arrived at Lauren's friend's house. A couple of my baseball buddies and I walked into a beautiful, huge home—marble floors, a huge living room, and, of course, a Mercedes in the driveway. Lauren timidly hugged me. She looked great in her red dress.

Lauren had dark black hair, big breasts, and was very sexy—but she wasn't Katie. As we were taking pictures, all I thought about was what Katie would look like at the dance and whether she had meant it when she had said that she would save a dance for me.

The dance was at the middle school, which was lit up magically. Lauren and I walked in together holding hands. "My hands are so sweaty," I said. She laughed and said that it was fine. I met up with my buddies in the corner and we all talked and laughed while the group of girls did the same thing. It was weird because, even though it was a dance, no one really danced.

I looked around anxiously for Katie; *where was she?* From a distance, I saw a couple walking together and laughing—Katie had arrived. I hated her boyfriend. *He's ugly*, I thought. She had on a blue dress with high heels that made her legs look so sexy. Her lips were covered in dark red lipstick, her smile lit up the whole room, and her pearly white teeth were perfect. I backed up in the corner, not knowing what to do; my heart sank and I panicked. *How was I going to dance with her?* She was an angel.

The night was coming to an end; Lauren and I had our last dance together. She kissed me on the lips and I blushed. It was my first kiss, but I had wanted Katie to be my first. Seeing Katie standing by herself, I walked over confidently after the song ended. "Hi, Katie," I said.

She smiled and said hello. I bit my tongue and asked if she had saved me a dance, crossing my fingers. She smiled intimidatingly and said, "Of course, Logan." I moved closer to wrap my arms around her, and my body immediately warmed up. It felt like I was in a sauna; as she wrapped her arms around me, I felt ecstatic. Her breasts were against my chest and my arms were holding her waist, as we slowly moved to the sound of love music. My whole world made sense when we danced; I forgot about my sick grandmother, my fighting parents, Jared's cut wrist—nothing else mattered.

CHAPTER 2

CALL MY NAME

The basketball court was filled with kids enjoying summer, girls in skimpy clothes, and hormones, everywhere. "Ice!" The ball gets passed; *cross over, pump fake, the shot, SWISH!* Summer basketball was one of the best times I've ever had. The girls would smile at me, and I felt like everyone knew my name.

I had separated from Jason and John during the summer of sixth grade; we no longer had much in common. They would watch from the sidelines as I would take the game-winning jump shot. My life seemed so clear to me now. If I kept playing and practicing basketball, maybe I could go pro and marry a beautiful wife and live in a huge mansion with fancy cars. The world was mine and I loved every moment of attention.

After summer league games, my basketball team would have pool parties at their parents' houses. We would all eat pizza and do backflips off the diving board. *Living the good life*, I thought. Even though I was from a family that was not wealthy, I blended in so well with wealth. My friends' parents loved me; maybe it was just because I was very athletic, but hey, I'd take it. The whole summer was amazing, from spending time with friends to playing pickup games at the schoolyard.

I had lost track of Katie, as I was beginning seventh grade and she had moved on to high school. I missed her, but knew that I would see her again when I went to high school; maybe by then, I would be on the varsity team and she would be my girl.

Seventh grade was not too much different, except it was nice no longer being the youngest in the school. My friends started hanging out with girls more often and the girls started to become more attractive to me. You could say that I was shy; there were a couple of older eighth-grade girls who, according to my friend Tim, thought I was cute. Even though my basketball game was on point, my social skills with girls were kind of lacking. After going to the dance with Lauren, we had split; I wasn't ready for a relationship, since I was only thirteen. The seventh-grade schoolwork was a little harder than it had been in sixth grade, but I didn't really struggle with it. There were a lot more dances now, though. We would all go to the dances in groups of friends and just stand around, looking cool.

Middle school was all about different trends, and, looking back, it makes me sick to remember how hard I tried to blend in. If one kid started wearing skateboarding clothes, soon the whole group would; if someone tried a new lunch sandwich, then the whole group would. That's when I started to notice different cliques. There were the jocks, which was the group that I fell into, and then there were nerds, stoners, skaters, hippies, goths, popular girls, promiscuous girls, and so on. Some of my friends from the team started to hang out with the promiscuous girls, and would always come back with lurid stories after hanging out under the bleachers. "Logan, this girl Meghan gave me a blowjob under the bleachers" or "Logan, she let me finger her." I was jealous after hearing these things, since it seemed like I was missing out.

Many times I tried to get the courage to ask a girl out, but just couldn't. I focused more on my basketball and baseball game, and decided that I was going to give it a little time. My friend Kevin tried to hook me up with Kelly in eighth grade. Kelly was known for pleasing all of the boys she went out with; she was a "giver." I was sitting at my desk as Kelly dropped a note off as she walked past to go to the bathroom. I looked around nervously at my classmates and teacher as my cheeks turned red. Of course, no one had seen anything, thank God. The paper was folded about ten times, and, as my teacher continued to talk about world history, I opened the letter slowly. With each unfold, my stomach tightened. As I got closer to the end, I started to see words appear:

Logan, I want your body. Will you go out with me?
YES or NO.

My mind was racing as my heart almost stopped. My palms got wet and my forehead started to glisten with sweat. I could barely swallow as I circled YES. I left the note on the end of my desk for her to grab. She walked by, smiling nervously as she smoothly grabbed the piece of paper. I looked over at her out of the corner of my eye and saw her opening it up so slowly, licking her lips and gently biting them and then smiling. She reached into her bag and took out lip gloss and unhurriedly put it on and blew me a kiss. I nervously smiled, and walked out to the bathroom when I noticed that my erection was harder than Stonehenge. I looked in the mirror, tucked my erection, and smiled as I headed back to class. The bell rang and she walked out with her friends while I walked out with mine. The day moved quickly because all I could think about was Kelly. I had a big basketball game that night and I knew Kelly was going to be there, so I was a bit nervous. *Had she seen me play?* I wondered.

The game was beginning at our home court. The crowd was fairly big; it consisted mostly of parents of players, and guys and girls that were hooking up with one another. The coach grabbed my shoulder to pull me in; I was looking in the crowd for Kelly and couldn't hear a word he was saying. The tipoff began as the ball was thrown out of bounds immediately. I grabbed it and inbounded it, looking for an open man. I passed the ball in and cut to the hoop to score an easy layup. Turning to run the other way, I saw Kelly walking in and laughing with her friends. *She looks so sexy*, I thought as I got back on defense. All I could imagine were her big lips pressed together as I played defense. Maybe it was the puberty starting to hit, but I couldn't focus at all as my defended player rushed passed me and scored easily. On offense, I could barely dribble the ball as I ran up the court, losing the ball out of bounds. Finally, I made it to the hoop, took the shot—*Foul!* I was heading to the line for two shots, thinking about Kelly again. This time, all I could imagine was her lips. *Wait a minute, what's going on?* My erection was starting. *Please not now; shoot, hurry, shoot.* I missed both free throws and was running back on defense as my erection was getting bigger and my cheeks grew redder.

TIMEOUT! I ran over to my coach and said that I had pulled something in my leg. *God, please get me through this game*, I thought. I sat out for the rest of the game, playing off my injury. *What a great game for Kelly to see*; I needed to hook up with her or this would happen forever. The game ended and we had barely won; my coach was having a small party afterward, pizzas and some parents and friends. As I walked out to find my parents in the crowd, Kelly stopped me and gave me a smile and hug. She said, "Are you okay?"

"Of course, I played off an injury," I answered. She smiled and said that she was going to get dropped off at the party and would see me there.

Mom, Dad, and Jared dropped me off at my coach's party. I said that I would get a ride back; I was at the age when I was embarrassed by my parents, so begged them to take Jared home. Opening the door, I saw my basketball team members laughing, eating pizza, and shooting hoops on the coach's mini arcade game. The girls were in one section and the parents were having drinks in the kitchen. Kelly ran up to me and squeezed me; I smiled, feeling the warmth of her body on me. "Logan!" Tim yelled. "We're going down to the basement, are you coming?"

In the basement the music was soft and the lights were dim. We all sat on the couch, watching TV and enjoying our victory tonight. My heart was racing, since I knew that Kelly was ready to hook up. Kelly grabbed my hand and walked me into the other room as my buddies from the team cheered and made sounds.

This was it; Kelly was all mine, and it was time to become a man. *SHIT! I don't know what I'm doing.* I had watched pornos, but I was not sure how I was supposed to do *that*.

Kelly and I were in a dark room in the basement and her lips were on mine as she slowly stuck her tongue in my mouth. She tasted like cherry lip balm and her hands gradually moved down to my belt buckle. I felt my pants being tugged down to the floor. I kicked them off when they reached the bottom and could feel the breeze of freedom circulating around my whole body as Kelly pleasured me. The night was young, and so were we; our lives were perfect.

I smiled the whole way home. Now I knew what my friends were talking about. I couldn't wait to tell the guys at school. School was a blast the next day; Kelly walked by, smiling at me as I confidently strolled with a twinkle in my eye as my buddies all jumped on my back.

"Are you going out with Kelly?" they asked.

"I'm not sure if I want a girlfriend yet, guys," I said. Summer could open so many doors, and I wanted to keep my options open. I was trying out for AAU basketball, which was a state team of all-stars from Massachusetts. This would show everyone how good I really was. Also, summer league basketball was starting in a couple weeks. Between those two commitments, I wanted to have time for hanging with the guys.

The Bay City Breakers' tryouts began the following week. Showing up was intimidating; I didn't know anyone and the kids were fast. They were good at dribbling, shooting, and passing. The drills the coaches made us do were different than the ones I was used to, and the defense was harder; I could barely get by some of these kids. Two hours of intense training and tryouts, and then I went home with my head down as I grabbed my basketball. My dad walked me out—he thought I did great and gave me some tips, and said not to worry. How could I not worry, though? I needed to make the team. The phone rang as I was grabbing a drink in the kitchen.

"Hello," I said.

"Hi Logan, it's Kelly." *Great, she couldn't have called at any worse time.* I was tired from tryouts, my phone was on a wire and wouldn't go beyond the kitchen, and my parents were right next to me.

"I gotta call you back later," I told her.

"Why?" she asked.

"I need to go; see you tomorrow," I said as I hung up. I felt bad, but this was not the time.

During dinner, my parents talked about their days like they actually cared. It seemed pretty obvious that they didn't, as my mom barely ate her food and my dad ate all of his food while nodding his head. *Is this what life comes out to?* Jared mashed his food around as my dad yelled at him to eat my mother's cooking; she, however, sweetly told my dad not to worry about it.

"Maria, he has to learn to finish the food given to him." My mom then asked how my tryouts went, and I nodded and said that they went okay. I had a feeling that the coach wouldn't call and that my dreams of being a pro basketball player were fading slowly. After dinner, I would usually play basketball in the yard, but tonight I felt like I never wanted to play again and just went to bed.

Yawning, I rolled out of bed on Saturday with a too-sore body, and walked out to the kitchen. My father had just gotten off the phone and called for my brother. "Jared!" he yelled. He arrived in the kitchen quickly, leaving his video games. My brother and I both respected my dad; he had always intimidated us, maybe because he was young and always in better shape than us.

"We're going to Lake Placid, New York for your hockey tournament. That was your coach," my dad told Jared. My brother got excited; this was his first time traveling for hockey. His team was doing really well and he would get a shot at playing against talented teams, like Canada. The trip was going to be for a weekend and would take place two weeks from then; we were thrilled.

Later in the evening, Mark McGowan from the Breakers called and my dad passed the phone over to me. "Logan, we liked the way you played and want to invite you to officially play for the Breakers. Practice starts Monday at seven and goes till nine." I jumped a foot after I got off the phone, screaming in excitement as I grabbed my old Spalding basketball and went out to the yard to dribble and shoot. I had so much energy just from that one call. This was going to be an amazing summer between AAU, Lake Placid, Kelly, and summer league; things were perfect.

"Four hours until we get there," my dad said. My parents had stopped for coffee and breakfast for us before we started the drive to Lake Placid. My coach was okay with me taking the weekend off to go to my brother's tournament. Kelly was pretty upset that I was leaving, but I still left. Jared and I were playing Gameboy and being kids in the back of the car, throwing food at each other, farting and laughing. The ride flew by for me, but I'm sure that for my parents it took forever. We arrived at the hotel and parked to check in.

It was a decent-sized hotel with a pool, Jacuzzi and a game room, so I was happy enough. I mean, besides going to Maine and New Hampshire, I had never been anywhere, so it was cool to be in New York. My dad and mom talked with other parents as Jared ran around the hotel with his hockey buddies. I felt like an outcast as I looked around for any kids my age, but didn't see any.

Jared had his first game at seven the next morning, followed by another game a couple of hours after that. I sat on the bed of the hotel room for a while, watching TV and being bored. I decided to walk down to the arcade and check it out; my mom had given me a room key and told me to be careful. As I went out, turning the corner, I saw a couple of kids in the arcade, mostly younger than me, and then I spotted two girls around my age— maybe a little older. I walked in, popped a quarter in a baseball arcade game, and started playing; I could hear the girls looking over at me and giggling. I glanced at them a couple times as they stared back, giggling some more. They came over after that, and asked me who I was and where I was from. They were here from Canada for the tournament. They then asked me which room I was in. I laughed and said 416, as they ran away, which was a bit confusing, but they were kind of cute. I finished the game and went back to the room.

KNOCK! KNOCK! KNOCK! "Who the hell could this be?" my dad and mom said.

"Is Logan there?" two girls asked as they giggled. My dad turned around with a huge smile as I blushed and my stomach dropped.

He said, "Oh, yes, Logan is right there; why don't you show him around?" and laughed.

"Dad, come on," I said reluctantly.

"Just go, Logan," he insisted.

"Fine," I said. They were so giggly and must have been like fifteen years old, while I was only thirteen.

They had a slight accent that was sexy; it was different from Kelly's Boston accent. It was very proper, which was kind of a turn-on for me. They brought me down to the swing set and both jumped on it, swinging, and laughing when they caught me blushing.

They asked if I have ever been to Canada, and I replied quickly with a "no." The wind was blowing gently and my legs were cold, but also very shaky as I could feel my knees buckling. *Why did they bring me here?* They slowly got closer to me, and one girl sat on the other's lap and kissed her on the lips gently as she looked over to see my reaction. My heart nearly exploded, and my knees felt like they were cemented into the ground.

"Logan?" they called me over and brought me in for a kiss. One of their mouths caressed my ear and the other was biting my lip—was this heaven? They slowly grabbed my leg and took control of the situation, making the night unforgettable.

I slept with my eyes open that night. It was hard to determine if I was dreaming about what just happened. I didn't even think it was worth telling anyone because nobody would believe me. My basketball buddies, Kelly . . . I was most certainly not telling her. I figured that I would keep this my little secret.

Morning arrived and I was so tired, but I must have had a smile that looked like I had won the lottery. My dad gave me a knowing look and smiled. My brother hopped on the ice, skating fast and shooting. The Canadian team was faster, bigger, and better, and even though my brother's team went zero-and-three in the tournament, I left feeling like a winner.

AAU had started and the first practice was brutal; the kids were faster, taller, and I was not the best one on the team, unfortunately. I was more like the sixth man after coach determined our roles in practice.

After only one weekend, I saw Kelly at my first summer league basketball game in town. She smiled and hugged me, but looked different. Later, after my game, I found out that she had been hooking up with another kid on my team. *How dare she*, I thought, *what a bitch!* Then I thought, *Well, technically, what had happened at Lake Placid was very similar, except I feel like I got more than just a hookup*. It made me realize how crappy middle school was, since no one knows what they really want. I was popular, so Kelly had liked me, and now another kid was becoming popular, so she liked him. I guess those weren't the girls for me.

I spent the rest of the summer playing basketball and going up to Cape Cod where my aunt and uncle rented a cottage. Cape Cod was amazing; when the tide would go out, I'd be afraid of all of the crabs and creatures, and my dad would put me on his shoulders and run through the water as I screamed. My whole family had spent each summer on Cape for the last couple of years. It was hard to see Papa up there; he was so fun when he wanted to be, but he would always worry about his wife, Eva—my Nana. She had gotten to the point where she didn't even know how to function anymore and didn't recognize her own family.

Summers on Cape Cod were probably the best times in my life. Nothing mattered, and the air up there was always different; maybe it was the smell of the seawater. After a long day at the beach, I would take a shower and throw on my comfortable shorts and tank top. We would all go out on the go-karts and trampolines, followed by ice cream for everybody. To end each night, we would all watch a movie, and the cousins usually fell asleep during the opening credits. The adults would then have a good time and act like kids; I'll never forget how peaceful life was back then.

That summer passed by as quickly as the rest, and I would soon begin my final year of middle school. The biggest downer in my life was my Nana, who was in the hospital and on her deathbed. My family had gathered at the Winchester Hospital, praying as we watched the woman who had struggled her whole life, but never once complained. She was only sixty seven years old. "Such a short life," my mother said as she cried on my father's shoulder. My eyes felt heavy as Jared and I stood in the back, confused with life. I was confused to see such a sweet woman lose her husband, kids, nephews, and nieces.

So Eva Verano passed away on that autumn night, and my mother stayed the night with her family as my dad, Jared, and I went home in silence. I hopped in my bed, staring up at the ceiling as my eyes squinted, and then I burst into tears, covering my face with the pillow.

The morning arrived and my mother was home at the dinner table, reading through college applications. She said that she was going to enroll in night classes to become a nurse. The tragedy of my Nana was devastating, but to see my mom finally having the courage to achieve her dreams was a breath of fresh air. She knew that becoming certified would be hard, but she accepted that she would do whatever it took to make it happen. She enrolled in Northern Essex Community College for a two-year nursing program. I could tell that she was frightened, but I think that the death of her mother had made her fearless in her own life.

Jared was entering fifth grade and seemed excited about it; he had tons of hockey friends and was popular. We stayed close, but he had his own friends and I had mine; we were always close, but we were no longer little kids playing in the yard anymore.

My first eighth-grade party was at Tim's house; even though his parents were always home, they never really seemed to pay too much attention to what he was doing. They lived in a beautiful million-dollar house with a basketball hoop, trampoline, and huge finished basement where all of us kids would hang out. The party mostly consisted of girls and guys making out or playing spin the bottle, hooking up, whatever young kids do. His seventeen-year-old brother would sometimes come downstairs with alcohol. Some of my friends would try it and did not really like it, and others, like me, would not even touch it. I was only fourteen, so there was no way I was going to drink; plus, why did I even need to? My life couldn't get better.

Besides regular weekend parties, I spent a lot of my time shooting hoops at the Thompson School across the street. It was my elementary school. I could spend hours there working on my crossover and imagining the fortune and fame that I would gain when I went to play in the NBA.

◉ ◉ ◉

The day that really made me realize that high school would be different was when I met Rory. "Hey, let's play one-on-one from a distance." He flicked a cigarette out of his mouth and opened his hands for the ball. *Who was this loser?* I wondered.

"I'm Rory, what's up man," he said. He told me that I didn't look familiar.

"I'm in eighth grade," I said.

"Oh, I'm in tenth; maybe I'll see you next year."

"You smoke, you choke." The commercial popped into my head. This kid was so winded that he couldn't even score a point, and he must have coughed every ten seconds. He said, "Nice game," as I beat him 11-3. When we ended the game, he lit up another cigarette. The smell was different this time though, and the paper burnt when he lit it. It smelled almost as if a skunk was passing by us; he asked if I wanted a hit.

I calmly said, "I'm good, man," as he laughed.

"What, you don't smoke?"

"No," I said, confidently.

"You will once you go into high school; I was the same way."

He hopped on his BMX bike and rode away as I whispered under my breath, *Loser*. No way would I ever smoke or drink.

"Mom," I yelled, smelling the meatloaf cooking in the kitchen. She was on the phone and looked worried; I saw her face pale as she leaned against the kitchen counter.

"Okay, bye; I'll let him know," she said into the phone.

"Who died?" I asked instantly, praying I was wrong. "I know that look."

Her voice shook. "Grammy passed away." *How could this happen?* Jared walked into the room with a confused, sad look. Dad was coming home any minute, and how could we tell him? The door handle turned and opened up slowly; Jared and I ran into the other room. "Hi, Clint," my mother said as he came in with his work boots and lunch box and hugged her.

He cautiously asked, "What's wrong? Maria, what the hell is it?"

"It's your mother—she passed away an hour ago." Jared and I turned the corner as my dad found out the news and, looking him in the eyes, for once I understood how young my father appeared. He looked like a young kid who had lost everything. We walked up to him and hugged him in the kitchen as he squeezed us all tightly and remained strong for us. I could tell that he wanted to cry, but, instead, he sadly stumbled into his truck and went for a drive.

I couldn't sleep much that night, tossing and turning, thinking about my father. As my eyes started to finally close, I heard a cry coming from downstairs. I ignored it at first, until it got louder. It had finally gotten so loud that my mother woke Jared and I to tell us that our father was crying downstairs and that we should go support him. I was scared; my father and I had always played baseball and basketball together, and we would watch TV together, but to see him cry touched me in a way that I didn't know how to handle. I turned the corner to find him, and he opened his arms as we hugged him. The feeling was hard to describe, but that night I saw that my father was so scared to lose his mother and I knew that one day this might be me. My eyes watered as tried to fall asleep.

The ceremony was sad; Grammy died from a heart attack just three weeks after my Nana passed away.

My mother had started classes and was having a difficult time. I understood, and with all of the events that had recently taken place, I didn't blame her. A couple of weeks later, I saw her crying, with her books scattered all over the table, and she told me that wanted to quit. "You can do it, Mom; I believe in you," I told her. "Be strong."

She smiled, closed her books, and said, "I know." For some reason, with all of the death around me lately, my heart had opened up to realize that we all needed to support our family if we wanted to make it through these hard times.

Eighth grade was flying by, especially with all that was going on in my life. All I could think about was spending the summer on the Cape again this year, even though it would be different. Everyone was getting older and growing up. I would be going into high school and Jared would be entering middle school; where had the time gone? AAU, baseball, and basketball didn't matter to me much anymore; next year, I needed a fresh start. *Keep practicing, Logan*, I said to myself, *keep practicing*.

Next year, I believed, I would see Katie again; she would be a junior and hopefully she had left her boyfriend. I also envisioned making the varsity teams during my freshman year in both basketball and baseball. Katie would come to my games wearing my varsity coat; she would be sitting in the stands watching me, smiling and blowing kisses.

My parents were so proud on the day their first son graduated from middle school. The ceremony was inside the gym where I had hit all my three-pointers, where I had had my first dance with Katie. My suit had been pressed and looked sharp for the ceremony. Jared, my dad, my mother, and my aunt and uncle joined us that day. The day was ecstasy, and I will never forget the feeling of walking up to the stage and shaking the principal's hand while the auditorium cheered my name.

Cape Cod was only a couple of weeks away, my uncle reminded me at my after-party. I was excited to ride the bumper cars and to jump on the trampolines. The smell of the beach, the feeling of sand getting stuck between my toes, and the look of my skin peeling from a sunburn doesn't sound like much, but for me, the Cape was completely relaxing. And, after all, I thought that I deserved it. If I had known that this would be my last trip to Cape Cod as a child, I would have cherished it even more.

CHAPTER 3

CHAIN OF EVENTS

I n three months I would be turning fifteen and, in about six months, my brother would be turning twelve; time was flying. So much had happened this year, but everything was starting over now that I was in high school.

I was average height, five-eight, which was surprising because my father was over six feet tall. I was slim but had reflexes like a cat. I weighed one hundred fifty-five pounds. My jeans fit loose but not baggy and I usually wore a baseball cap. My hair was gelled perfectly as it stood up and curved to the side. I had an infectious laugh; people liked to be around me.

The first day arrived, and my dad dropped me off at the front of the building. Embarrassed, I hopped out and looked immediately for my friends. Intimidated by the seniors and juniors and realizing that I didn't recognize anyone I knew, I wondered, *Am I at the right school?*

"Logan," *Thank God*; there was my friend, Tim, from basketball. We both looked nervous. A girl gently brushed by my elbow, and glanced back quickly, and then moved along. *She didn't even notice me*, I thought, and then it hit me that this was my love, Katie. Was it possible that she had forgotten me already?

The bell rang as I looked at my schedule; I had no clue where anything was. I wandered the halls, seeing only faces of strangers before noticing a couple of buddies who looked familiar. *Was that John?*

Jason and John, however, had both gotten into private schools that year. Jason attended Phillips Academy in Andover, Massachusetts and John went to Saint John's. These were both high-class schools for wealthy families. My mom and dad worked hard just to keep a roof over our heads.

Sitting in class, all I could think about was basketball tryouts later that day. *Would I be good enough? Would things be like they were in middle school?* I wasn't concerned about my classes too much, since I always managed to study hard and maintain mostly B's—I wasn't a genius, but I was definitely not dumb.

Lunch came quickly after a couple of class periods, and I walked in nervously searching for a place to sit. I walked over to the guys on my basketball team and smiled, grabbed a couple slices of pizza, and sat down. *Deep breath*, I thought, *hopefully now I can just sit here all year and not have to worry about moving seats.* I wanted to establish myself in the "jock" category. At the table, there were a couple of new faces, people from different towns and states who had moved into the area. Apparently, some of them played sports and so they sat with us.

One girl was amazing; Gina had jet-black, long, curly hair and big curves. She was dark-skinned, maybe Italian. She had dark, deep eyes with mascara applied almost excessively, but on her, it was just enough. Then, of course, my love Katie was sitting three tables down, laughing. *It's just a matter of time before I make the varsity team and ask her out.*

I decided to walk home after school with a couple of friends who lived on the way. It was a bit longer walk than I would have liked, but I wanted the freedom and wanted to avoid being embarrassed by having my mom pick me up. There was a long overpass connected from the schoolyard over the highway, where kids could walk over the highway without having to cross traffic. At the end of the overpass there was always a group of juniors who would be smoking cigarettes, wearing loose jeans, and comparing piercings and tattoos. They were just punks, if you asked me, not the kids I wanted to hang out with. My buddies and I would walk by quietly, trying to avoid them; of course, we weren't nerds so they always left us alone and picked on weaker kids. I always asked myself, *What had to have gone wrong in their lives to lead to them sinking so low?*

I got home that day and grabbed my basketball to start practicing my jump shot. Tryouts were not far away, and I needed to make Varsity in order for Katie to notice me. Jared got home a little after me with a couple of new buddies and they ran around the house, laughing and playing video games. His friends seemed pretty cool: they played sports like Jared and were overall decent kids.

My mother was studying in the house and had to stop once Jared and his friends came over; they were so loud that I didn't know how she got any work done. Dad arrived home a couple of hours later and kicked everyone out as my mom served dinner. We sat down and discussed our days; I described high school as a movie and Jared said that middle school was okay. My mom started to clear the table and returned to studying while my dad went down to the basement to focus on wood carvings and other projects. I was never really into it, but Jared would spend hours down there with him. I was closer to my mom and would share my whole day and my dreams with her after she finished studying.

Basketball tryouts arrived and I was ready. Coach Mangella was about six-five and skinny like a string bean, with a perpetually mean, serious look. He introduced himself to all twenty freshmen.

We scrimmaged to start; he split us up into two teams. It was different than normal tryouts. The first time that I got the ball, my palms were so sweaty I had lost the ball. *Shit! Not a good start*, I thought as I nervously ran back. "Okay, defense," I said, "Let's go!" *Damn.* The kid on the other team ran right past me; I was frustrated that I had been fooled, allowing him to score.

"Logan, sub out with Tim," Coach Mangella said. *How am I playing so badly? I practice more than anyone here.* I took a five-minute break, shaking my knees on the bench while waiting to get back in the game and prove myself.

"Okay, let's do this; pass the ball!" *Crossover, behind-the-back three-pointer! Swish!*

"Ice," I heard as I looked into the bleachers to see the seniors I had known from fifth grade calling my name. I smiled and ran back on defense. *That's all I needed*, I thought, *just a little boost.*

"Steal by Michaels, breakaway layup! SCORE!" I looked over at Coach Mangella, but he showed no emotion and didn't give me much credit. The scrimmage was over and I was pretty happy with my performance. The tryouts ended with a couple of dribbling and shooting drills until I heard the whistle blow. Everyone gathered around Coach Mangella and took a knee.

"Team," he said, "Twelve of you will make the team; the roster will be in the gym tomorrow at three. Also, all freshman—there will be no spots on varsity, no matter how good you are because the varsity team already has too many people." My heart sank, but I understood and thought that maybe I could show him how good I was in my games and make the team later.

◎ ◎ ◎

School was a drag the next day. I didn't pay any attention to my classes, and all I could think was, *Is it three yet?* Running to the gym immediately, I saw Coach Mangella posting the roster.

I stood behind most of the kids, waiting until it cleared out. You could tell right away who had made the team and who hadn't just by their expressions. In the third row down, I saw *Logan Michaels*; my eyes glowed. Also posted was the schedule for practice, which would be every day after school at four. It was exciting to be able to travel to compete against rival teams and to see what kind of other talent was out there.

Arriving home that night, I saw that my mother was crying at the table again. My dad seemed to ignore her. Her books were scattered and I learned that she had failed her first test. I couldn't bear to see the sadness in her face; she wanted to succeed so badly, but had to provide for two sons at the same time. My father would always go downstairs after they got in a fight, and it seemed to me that they were separating, but I told myself that it must be a phase. People say that happiness doesn't ˅ have anything to do with money, but it seemed like money was dividing my parents. Jared seemed clueless.

My weekends when I was fifteen were pretty simple. My friends and I would go to the high school football games at Hayers Stadium. Everybody would be at the games, and it made me want to be a football star. I hoped that the basketball and baseball games would attract this many people. Most of the seniors and older kids would sneak in alcohol and would drink behind the stadium fence while the hippies would smoke marijuana under the bleachers. Girls and guys would make out and hook up in the woods, and fights would erupt between guys from rivaling towns, which the cops would usually have to break up.

Friday nights were when all of the parties happened, usually hosted by football players. I always wondered where the parents were when these parties happened. I mean, I could barely talk to a girl on the phone without my whole family overhearing the conversation. I'd usually hang out with my friends and watch the games; I never tried marijuana or alcohol. I thought of Rory, the kid that I had met last year, and reflected on how he predicted that I would be into drugs and alcohol. *Screw him*, I thought.

My first real high school party was after one of the football games against neighboring Methuen. We had won the game and there was going to be a huge party afterward at the home of one of the linebackers. Apparently, his parents were always away on business trips, leaving him with his older brother, who was in college. His brother would buy kegs of beer for the team and they would celebrate, getting wasted after every game. Most of the high school's student body would show up at his mansion of a house to party on a regular basis.

A couple of my basketball buddies and I were driven there that night by some of the older kids. I was pretty nervous while walking into the party, since I had never been to this kind of scene. There were kids smoking marijuana right outside the house; girls were falling down and yelling, and the football players were doing keg stands. It was tough to understand what was happening because I didn't drink or smoke, and neither did my friends.

"Ice!!" I heard from a distance as one of the seniors grabbed me and said, "This is Ice!" He introduced me to a couple of his buddies and put a beer in my hand. I laughed and smiled and nervously faked a sip of beer. I put the can of Bud Light to my lips, tilted my head, and then spit the beer back into the bottle slowly. I didn't want them to see that I was a dork. If my mom knew that I was drinking at a party, she would have killed me. As the night went on, it was becoming harder to pretend that I was drunk. I was walking outside to dump my beer into the woods when I heard my name called.

"Logan!"

I turned to see a girl standing there, looking confused and tipsy. I squinted my eyes to see that it was Kelly, smiling, with a beer in her hand. She jumped on me and started to kiss me, and

I could smell the alcohol on her breath.

"Hey, how are you?" I said. She kissed me and started to grab me as I became hard and I began to breathe heavily. "Kelly, you're drunk," I said.

She responded, "So what?" as she licked my ear and kissed my neck. *It feels so good, though,* I thought to myself. I imagined Katie being the one who was licking my ear, as I kissed Kelly back and started to slip my tongue into her mouth.

We made our way to the garage as we made out. Her breath smelled like beer, but my hands caressed her breasts as she grabbed me. My hands started to slip down her skirt. It was warm and wet as she moaned and breathed heavily, sighing.

"Logan," I heard.

Shit. "Who is that?" I asked.

"We need to leave; my mom's picking us up, and the football players are wasted."

"Coming," I said as my penis went soft again. "Bye, Kelly," I said as she tugged on my arm, trying to get me to stay. "I gotta go; I'll talk to you Monday, bye." *Great party,* I thought to myself, and I think I was the only one who hadn't been drinking.

◉ ◉ ◉

Monday arrived, and Kelly walked by me in the hallway. As I raised a hand to wave hello, she completely ignored me. *What the hell,* I thought to myself; did she even remember what had happened? Tim then came up to me and said, "Did you hear about Kelly and Josh?"

"No," I said.

"They hooked up Friday night after you left." I slammed my locker and walked to class. Apparently she would have hooked up with anyone, since she had been so drunk. *Whatever, I'm going to focus on basketball now,* I thought, *I don't like her anyway.*

So, Josh knew that Kelly and I had a thing going on, and he had hooked up with her anyway. I tried not to think about being stabbed in the back by Josh, especially since he was a junior and a lot bigger than me. Practice came and I was missing shots, dribbling poorly and just losing focus overall. Coach Mangella pulled me aside and told me to sit while Tim took my spot. Tim was good, but he wasn't as good as I was; he had a nice jump shot and was decent at dribbling, but he never practiced and had a poor attitude. I couldn't let this situation affect me—I had practiced way too hard to let one girl ruin this. The week continued like this, with Tim and me switching in for one another; on some days he did well and on some days I did well.

The first game arrived, and Coach Mangella read off the starting lineup. "Tim," he said, "You're at shooting guard; Logan, you will be the sixth man until you pick things up." My lip quivered, but I kept a strong face. The team put their hands in the huddle as I felt like my whole world was crashing down.

Tim and I split time during the game, but I really wanted to start. My parents could tell how bummed out I was while I sat on the bench—I just wasn't myself. My confidence was shattered and I felt depressed. First, Kelly had hooked up with Josh, and now I was not even starting on my *freshman* team.

My parents drove me home as I quietly sat in the backseat, listening to my dad and mom yell at one another about work, my mom's classes, and bills. Jared no longer came to my games; he would usually hang out at his friends' houses.

For the rest of that week, I completely blocked out Kelly and anything that would have a negative effect on me. A week later, Coach Mangella announced the starting lineup and I heard my name get called to start.

Hands in the air, I yelled, "GO KNIGHTS!" as I ran out onto the court for my first starting game in high school. The feeling was surreal when I heard my name, "Ice," being called by the varsity guys; my head could have floated away. Halftime arrived and as I was walking off the court, I saw Kelly and Josh kissing. *Fuck them,* I said to myself.

The next day in school, there was an announcement to the freshman Knights team for winning their game. "And the Player of the Game, scoring twenty-five points and seven assists, is Logan Michaels."

A strong wind flushed through my soul with feelings of ecstasy. Things were good for me again, and maybe Katie had heard the news. People started to recognize my name as the season continued like this, and jocks, hippies, cute girls, and even teachers would congratulate me on my awesome game.

School was pretty easy because the entire teaching staff gave me a break on homework, so I maintained B's throughout the first couple of semesters while I was playing basketball. I tried to focus on my game instead of messing around with girls; I didn't want to get hurt again. Plus, finding out soon afterward that Katie wasn't into me made me want to just avoid girls altogether. She had a boyfriend who was a junior, and they had been together since our days in middle school. *I need to let it go, I guess.*

Maybe next basketball season I could make varsity, but until then the season was over. Baseball was starting soon and I was both excited and nervous to see what I could do. My freshman coach had made quite the impression on me when I first met him. He was a history teacher for sophomores, so I might possibly have him as a teacher the next year.

One day, as I was stretching on the high school field to loosen up my arm, a man began to walk over. He had white wavy hair, and must have been sixty years old. He was wearing khaki pants with New Balance shoes, and he had an old flannel shirt, half untucked, which was covered by a black bubble vest. He pushed his glasses up on his face as he flipped the page in his book and continued to read. He shut the book when he got onto the field, and said, "I'm

Mr. Hillfield; let's begin with warmups." I really didn't know what to think of him, but, for some reason, I liked him.

"Catfish Hunter," a voice said as my shoulder was grazed. Mr. Hillfield was right behind me, smiling with his yellow teeth. "I heard a lot about you; let's see what you can do." He put me on the mound and called over a catcher as I dug my cleats into the mound. I had been practicing my pitches for months with my dad and threw in two perfectly accurate fastballs right down the middle. Mr. Hillfield smiled. "Okay, Logan, let's try the curveball." I remembered where my father told me to line up my fingers, and how to twist my wrist as I released. *Here goes nothing,* I thought. *SMACK!* Into the catcher's glove. I had the attention of the whole team at tryouts as he asked me to throw my curveball again. *SMACK!* "Wow," he said, "Looks like we have our starting pitcher." My curveball broke perfectly into the lower corner of the catcher's mitt.

In my first game I pitched a two-hitter with ten strikeouts. I was Mr. Hillfield's golden boy; he spent all the time he could coaching me. At this point in time, I wasn't sure whether I was better at basketball or baseball. The next day in school, I heard the announcement about the freshmen boys' first win, with a "Mr. Logan Michaels, Player of the Game." As I walked into my classes throughout the day, my teachers called me "Mr. Superstar," and I smiled and sat back in my chair like I was king.

Mr. Hillfield would see me in the hall and yell out, "Catfish!" Everyone would turn, and I'd smile, embarrassed. I don't know why he liked me so much, but I liked him, too. Catfish Hunter was a Hall of Fame baseball pitcher who had played in major league baseball from 1965 until 1979. It was a name no one could forget.

By the end of my freshman year, I decided that high school had its ups and downs. I had focused on my two main sports and had become known as an all-star on both teams.

My mother and father were very proud. They needed a bright

spot in their lives as they continued to struggle personally and financially.

I had wrapped up my baseball season with a perfect pitching season of five wins and zero losses. My curveball was the talk of the team, and Mr. Hillfield couldn't wait to see what I would do the next year. He told me that I was special and that I was going places, and I truly believed him.

◎ ◎ ◎

That summer, we had to skip my wonderful relaxation on the Cape for the first time. My parents just couldn't afford to take the time off from work and my mother was working hard to get her nursing degree. My AAU basketball was canceled because it was too expensive, which was kind of a drag, but I still had summer league basketball, which was free at the community center.

Summer league was incredible; I loved the feeling of freedom from school and getting together with my basketball buddies to play on the courts outside. But it was a little depressing to see my friends go away to the Bahamas or to other tropical islands with their families. I had never been further than Cape Cod, and I had thought that was amazing—I couldn't imagine what Bermuda or Costa Rica was like. *Maybe when I become a famous athlete, I can buy a house down there and retire to the perfect life with a beautiful wife*, I thought, *but until then I guess I'll need to grind it out.*

Summer flew by that year and I was happy. Most kids never wanted summer to end, but I wanted to get back into my basketball season. Sports seemed to keep my mind busy, and I never let it wander onto other things. I was also excited because I would be turning sixteen this year, and was close to getting my learner's permit. I had no clue how I would afford a car, and I realized that I would probably have to get a job soon. Some days, I would work with my dad doing construction, but I never really liked working with my hands. Plus, it was tough to find time to work while playing sports.

My sophomore year had started and, by the time I would wake up for school, my dad had already left for work. My mother would wake up early to drive Jared and me to school, and even though she was very tired, she never missed a day. A lot of my friends from basketball and baseball were in different classes, and I got paired up with a lot of kids who were into the party scene—not sports.

"What's up, man?" I heard during class. I turned to see a face that was familiar, unfortunately.

"Oh, hey, what's going on? I thought you were a senior," I said.

"Nah, man, I got held back in this stupid math class twice."

As his eyes looked sleepy, it became quite obvious that he was high on something. "Rory," he said. I remembered him from the park that day. How could I forget the kid who had told me that I would one day be into drugs? He said that he had seen me play ball and that I was incredible. "We should chill sometime."

I brushed him off. "Yeah, sure."

Class ended and I went off on my own separate path, dreading spending a semester in class with him. He was one of those kids who would always try to drag you into a conversation while the teacher was actually looking at you, making us both look bad; it drove me nuts.

Coach Lasell ran the junior varsity team. He was the one I would be trying to impress at tryouts. For me, making the team was an automatic, but maybe this year I could get onto varsity, now that a lot of the seniors had graduated.

Tryouts started off well, as we did some passing and shooting drills, and then did a scrimmage halfway through tryouts. Right then, a vision came to me that really messed up my game: I couldn't hit a single shot, my hands were sweating, and my heart was racing so fast that I thought I was going to die. In the vision, I had so vividly seen my mother sitting alone at the dinner table, crying, and I didn't know what this meant, but it hit me in the hardest way possible. All I could think about was what was happening at home; things had been unsteady for a year now, and it seemed the fighting never stopped.

Tryouts ended and my coach didn't look impressed. I knew he shouldn't have been, since I had not played to my full potential. My dad picked me up from tryouts in his old Dodge Caravan. It was maroon-colored and had a sliding door that Jared opened for me, so I hopped in the car, frowning. My dad was quiet, and he asked me how tryouts went as he bit his nail with a concerned look on his face.

"Your mother and I have to talk to you and Jared."

When we got home, we walked in the house and I saw the same image that had hit me during basketball tryouts—my mother was sitting there at the table, but she wasn't crying. She looked almost as if she had finally given up on love forever; the look on her face was that of a girl whose life had been hard, and that of a woman whose adulthood was a lie. My throat closed up at the table because either someone had died again, or my parents were no longer in love, and either one would change life for all of us.

CHAPTER 4
TEARS ON A BLUE COLLAR

J ared and I had seen my mother cry a lot over these years. There was a certain pain behind her dark brown eyes that we couldn't explain. They were filled with love, sadness, and uncertainty. Until the night my mother told us that she and my father were getting divorced, I always imagined things weren't that bad.

My mother had never really told me and Jared about her past or childhood until that unforgettable night that changed my life. My father drove off to a hotel for the night because he couldn't face the reality of me and Jared not living with him anymore.

Jared and I went upstairs to our rooms and closed the doors. We were only separated by a piece of thin sheetrock, but I swear I could feel his thoughts because they were similar to mine: uncertainty, sadness, and denial of what was happening and how it happened so quickly. We then heard a shallow, low knock on our doors to hear our mother's voice: "Boys, are you okay? Can

I come in?"

My mother's tears had finally ended, but her eyes looked uneasy. She had smeared mascara and was wearing sweatpants and one of my father's T-shirts. "Boys I need to tell you about my childhood and how your father and I met."

Jared and I sat on the edge of my bed; my throat was dry and my heart felt like it was in my stomach as my mother finally let go and told us everything, beginning with herself as a young girl.

"In 1973, my father had returned from the Vietnam War to his hometown of Stoneham, Massachusetts—where he and my mother raised two boys and two girls. From the outside, our home and family looked picture-perfect. Your grandfather drove a simple green Chevy Impala to work every day while your Nana, who didn't drive, always managed to get a ride to work. George and Tim, their sons, your uncles, as well as their eldest daughter, my sister Catherine, were well into their teens, but the youngest, me, was just turning nine when life changed for me.

"I was just as feisty as I was sweet. And, my strong personality was almost all that I had to help me weather the storm inside our modest home. You see, my father, the veteran, was severely depressed.

"Our house must have been the smallest on the block. To me it felt like living in a mental institution. What others called 'home,' I called 'trying to survive.'

"Times got worse over the years leading up to when I was in middle school. We never had food, clothes, or heat. Most nights, I would cry myself to sleep because I was always alone. I used to have a backpack adorned with my name, but after years of wear and tear, the 'Maria' stitching had worn off and it now just said, 'Ma.' Middle school was a time when everyone wanted to become accepted and to blend in, but all I remember is feeling outcast and embarrassed. Middle schoolers aren't the nicest people in the world, suffice to say.

"I never understood why we struggled financially, because both of your grandparents worked twelve-hour shifts almost every day. Your uncles looked after me, and your aunt was taking care of herself and was rarely home. My mother worked in a factory as an assembly line employee. I rarely got to see her; she worked so hard for such little return.

"I remember when the family came crashing down. It was late at night when they took my daddy away while he was yelling and crying, looking lifeless in a straitjacket. I watched as his frail body was placed on the stretcher, which broke my tiny heart.

"My dad was diagnosed with bipolar disease and severe psychosis, which he had been living with every day since the war. After returning home weeks later from the mental institution, things seemed back to normal. Until it happened again. That was the pattern we dealt with, his debilitating suffering.

"Most nights when Dad got home from work he didn't want to be seen. I'll never forget his face the night he actually flipped out. He was expressionless, but I could sense that he was overwhelmed, tired, sad, angry, and confused—everything was in his blank stare. I came out of my room, which consisted of a bed, bare walls, and holes in the cracked wooden floors. I didn't know what to think; I was home alone with Dad, and had no one to turn to for help. I picked up my journal from my small bed, held it close to my chest, and walked up to him. I asked him 'What happened, Dad?'

"They laid him off. After ten years of seventy-hour workweeks, they let him go.

"I remember telling him that it would be okay. That night at the dinner table, my whole family was home and no one could eat a bite; we were all too sad for my father. When my mother said that she would increase her hours to pay for the bills, I thought about how physically impossible that was, but remained quiet.

"Weeks passed and my father hadn't gotten off the couch.

Weeks turned into months and my father was slipping into an even deeper depression. I remember starting seventh grade and my friends making fun of me. They'd tell me, 'We saw your father walking down the street with a hood on, talking to himself and playing with his beard.' I would cry myself to sleep every night.

"I came home from school one day and saw police cars and ambulances surrounding my house. I bolted to my front door, and flung it open like a bat out of hell. I saw a man I didn't recognize run out the doorway as if he was being chased. He jumped off the porch and was immediately tackled by an officer. The man who looked up at me had lost eyes, a scruffy beard, and dirty clothes. My eyes welled up as I realized that my father was not the man he used to be.

"The proud war veteran was long gone; he was no longer the happy man with a wife and loving family; he had been destroyed by life and looked as if he were possessed. I looked around at that moment and saw a home that was dirty, small, and ultimately lonely. One of my brothers turned to me and said, 'Happy birthday, Maria.'

"Dad was admitted to the mental hospital exactly six months after he was laid off. The company claimed he was not eligible for health insurance or paid time off to cope with his mental illness. I don't know if it was the war that broke my father or if it was the fact that his decent life was stolen from him by a pink sheet of paper. Maybe both.

He returned home after a month of being on lithium and God knows what else, and walked through the door, soulless. This was not my father. As I cried on my small bed, I watched the cockroaches scatter on the floor and listened to my older siblings scream at each other. My mother was working seventy hours a week and we were still dirt poor.

"After Dad's many hospitalizations, life at home became a little easier to deal with. While I was middle school, the kids on the bus had mercilessly made fun of my father and of how poor we were. Now that did not happen anymore; I had discovered that if I faked a smile and didn't let anyone see my emotions, they would think my life was great. I decided that I wouldn't show anything but confidence because otherwise, I would probably break down.

"My friends didn't know that every day, I would come home from school to find my father screaming and crawling on the floor, hallucinating. I walked into my room one day to see that all of the pictures on the walls had holes cut into them where the eyes used to be because my father had thought they were staring at him. He was at his worst at night. My father would smash my door, trying to break it down. I would sit on my bed, crying and hoping for him to go away as the pounding grew harder and louder. And each morning, I put on my smiley face.

"Time and again, my father would be extracted from the house in a straitjacket. And, after a month or so away he would return, walking the streets with a hood over his head. Over time, he had destroyed all the furniture and burned to ashes everything else in the place. Now, we had nothing in our house besides our beds. There were times I wanted to go to sleep and never wake.

"I am telling you all of this, boys, so you can understand my emotions. I never wanted you to suffer emotionally the way I did. I never wanted us, as a family, to suffer financially the way we have. You father left because I don't want you boys exposed to the anger and hurt that I lived through. I am tired of you boys seeing me cry.

"As a girl I suffered with depression. I still do. I think that my depression took a toll on your father. He couldn't make me happy, nothing could—except having you boys. Separating from your dad will help him in the long run. I am hoping it will help me as well."

CHAPTER 5

SOMEBODY WAKE ME

T he divorce was very hard on the whole family. Dad was moving out to get his own place while Jared and I would look after my mother. My father was moving right down the street in town into a one-bedroom apartment, but not seeing him every day after he came to our house from work and on Sundays watching football kind of hurt. I tried to keep strong for Jared; he was only twelve and too young to really know what was happening here.

I knew that my parents fought over money and such, but I never thought it would affect their love for each other. My parents had been together for almost twenty years; they had spent their adolescence together, had raised two beautiful kids, and had spent warm nights together on Cape Cod... and now, in the blink of an eye, it was all gone. *I am a product of a divorced family and now another statistic,* I thought to myself, and I grew angry at my parents.

At school, it was hard to walk down the hallways with a happy face. I kept it a secret from everyone that my perfect family was not so perfect. I walked down the hall slowly, thinking of Jared and what he might be thinking, wondering if he even cared.

The first time my father picked me up after basketball practice, after they broke the news to us, was weird. I couldn't even look him in the eye; it was almost like we were strangers because he was not living in the house. He had Jared in the back seat and I sat in the front and told him about practice.

Jared and I would stay over at his one-bedroom apartment a couple of nights a week. He would cook us hot dogs and beans—just what you would expect from a bachelor in his mid-thirties. Silently, we'd watch TV from his small couch, and we never really talked about the situation or the fact that he and my mother were no longer in love. He bought another single bed so Jared and I didn't have to share the couch. Some nights, I would think about how happy our family had been, and how everything was over now; my life was broken.

● ● ●

The basketball season would be starting soon, but my mind was so unfocused; it was hard to play with the whole situation at home. Coach Lasell started to lose faith in me because I wasn't performing to my "full capability," he said. All I could think about was my lonely mother, studying all night to better herself.

Coming home from practice was tough, because sometimes Jared wouldn't be home and my mother would be studying while also trying to cook dinner and figure out where Jared was. My little brother seemed to be handling the situation differently; he tried not to be home ever—maybe avoiding the house helped him forget how our lives used to be when we were a full family.

No more family dinners, so I would usually eat and watch

TV while Jared would eat at the table, and my mom would pick at the food later, once she cleared our plates and did the dishes. No more nights of family movies with Dad sipping a cold Sam Adams. At times, I would wonder what my father was doing. Was he sitting in his apartment by himself? Did he enjoy being alone, without his family? Thinking of this often made me depressed. I had never struggled from depression until now; I mean, I had had my dark days when basketball didn't go my way, but now I was finally starting to see the dark in the world.

School frustrated me, especially when a teacher would call my name. I just wanted to be left alone, and as they stared at me, waiting for the answer, I would think, *Leave me alone.* Then I would reply, "I don't know the answer."

Coach Lasell lost faith in me, and for our first game I was on the bench. He would put me in as the sixth man, which was not the worst. But my star had faded; I was no longer the revered "Ice" who scored twenty points a game. I didn't care too much, though; after all, I had no one supporting me in the crowd. My mother was at night classes taking finals, my father didn't show up to most games, fearing that he might see my mother, and Jared was at a friend's house doing God knows what. I had no one to impress. My heartthrob Katie paid me no attention, either. I had been deluded to think she ever would.

After each game, I would usually need to get a ride home from my buddies. It was kind of annoying to watch all of my friends hop in the cars with their families. I would sit quietly in the backseat, listening to how happy their parents were, driving their Mercedes and living comfortably, and it made me sick. I would just smile and thank them for the ride, but secretly, I hated them. Or did I really hate my parents for splitting us up?

Two months into the basketball season and I was officially on the bench; Tim had replaced me as the starting shooting guard. I had too much hate in my heart to care about basketball anymore. I would only see my father on the weekends and I didn't know who he was anymore. Jared and I would see each other after school and would walk past each other like we were strangers. He would always be out with his friends and it was hard for my mom to keep an eye on us because she was either selling Mary Kay products or studying for school.

My sixteenth birthday arrived and it was the first time since the split that I saw my family together again. It was awkward to see my Dad walk in wearing his new jeans and blazer and sporting a sharp haircut; he looked younger each day. It was almost as though he was happier without a real family. Maybe Mom was right: *Maybe they are happier apart*. It made me depressed to think that maybe we were all just a mistake and that maybe I was never supposed to be here.

Jared and I sat at the table as my parents awkwardly asked one another how they were doing. My mother, of course, had a smile on, but I could tell it was fake and that my father's was fake, too. I just wanted to get out of the house as soon as possible and not look back; it made me sick to be around them when I knew that it was all a lie.

After my lonely "sweet sixteen," I just wanted to leave the house. My dad pulled away and Jared went to a friend's house as my mother studied for her last final exam. Whenever I would get depressed, I would walk over to the Thompson School to shoot hoops, which is what I did that night. I would shoot and think of last year and how happy I had been and how things had changed so much. I could play for hours out there, just thinking about life in general and how I desperately wished I could change it.

"Logan?" I heard from the distance. "What's up, man? It's Rory."

We started to shoot hoops and chatted as we played; I don't know if I was feeling vulnerable, but I started talking about my parents getting divorced and how much it sucked. He told me that his parents were divorced and that it sucked for him, too, but that allowed him way more freedom now and he loves it.

"I never thought of it that way," I said.

"Listen, man, I have a hoop at my house, so if you ever want to come chill at my place and watch TV or something...."

Maybe Rory wasn't as bad as I had thought; I mean, he actually understood what I was going through here, unlike my other friends with perfect lives and perfect families.

"Yeah, man, that sounds good," I replied, this time meaning it.

I saw Rory in school over the next week and we started to chat more and more, laughing in class together. The teachers had to tell me to stop talking in class instead of Rory, but I kind of brushed them off disrespectfully. I'd started to shy away from my basketball friends because they didn't know what I was going through and I didn't even bother to explain it, knowing they wouldn't understand. Practice was boring, since I wasn't a starter and was slowly becoming a permanent fixture on the bench; my heart was not in the game anymore.

The first time I went to Rory's house was later that week. He only lived two blocks away, so I would walk across the Thompson School yard and cut through a couple of neighborhoods, through the Little League field I used to play on, and his house was right there. It was a medium-sized, but old, and it had a couple of broken-down cars in the driveway along with a crappy old basketball hoop that wasn't even regulation size.

He also lived with his mother; she was an older woman who smoked cigarettes and looked as if she had lost hope in this world. I prayed that my mother wasn't going to look like that one day. We played basketball outside in his small driveway. He had a couple of Adirondack chairs out in the backyard that we would sit in. His buddy Tyler came over, and when I first met him, I thought, *He's a short, sarcastic little punk.* He was hunched over and had a cigarette in his mouth at all times. He joined us and then sat on the chair texting on his cell phone.

"Rory, do you know anyone who has weed?" he asked. I laughed, trying to look cool, even though I never had tried it before. Tyler asked me if I smoked and I told him, "No, I'm not into that." He laughed at me, lit up another cigarette and then offered me one as Rory lit one up, too.

"Can I have the lighter?" I asked. They didn't have to persuade me at all; *Screw it,* I thought, there was no reasoning behind my choice, I'd just wanted to try one. *COUGH!* After I had inhaled my first drag, I said, "What a terrible taste; these things are disgusting." They laughed as I inhaled another drag slowly. It felt good this time; my head felt light and my eyes shut a little bit. *What a wonderful feeling.* I was hanging out with a couple of guys who never judged me and who came from similar backgrounds; I didn't have to impress them with a jump shot or curveball. They understood me for me, and I liked that.

Later that night, I headed home after spraying on some of Rory's cologne, so I wouldn't smell like cigarettes. My mother had a smile on her face that I hadn't seen for a while. "I passed," she said modestly.

My mother had achieved her dream of getting her nursing license while going through her divorce and trying to raise two young men. I was so proud of her, and things started to look up again after the news. It made me realize that if my mom could be this strong, why couldn't I get back into basketball on the starting lineup again? *Come on, Logan; you're stronger than this.*

Her graduation ceremony was planned for right before Christmas at Northern Essex Community College, which had one of the most rigorous nursing programs around. I wondered what my dad would think; even though they had been separated for a couple of months, would he care to show up?

Jared and I visited him the next day and gave him the good news and told him how proud we were of Mom. He smiled and said, "I know, I was with her." I'm not sure if he was truly happy for her, but he looked like he was.

● ◉ ◎

Over the next couple of weeks, I was focused on basketball and was making progress toward the starting lineup. The season was almost over and Coach Lasell appreciated my effort, even though I still wasn't there yet. I figured that I had all summer and the rest of the year to practice for my junior year, and that I would come back ten times better than before.

Rory, Tyler, and I would hang out a couple days a week, late after basketball practice. It would be dark out when I'd walk through the fields and through the neighborhoods to get to Rory's house. They would smoke marijuana every day, whether it was with a joint or out of a bowl. They still couldn't get me to smoke weed after asking many times, but they never forced me into it. I would smoke cigarettes with them here and there, but I wasn't addicted to nicotine.

December arrived and my mother wore her white nursing gown and cap. She looked so happy and beautiful. Her dad was there in his green sweatshirt, along with my uncle and aunts. My uncle looked very happy for Mom, as he breathed heavily and shook his knees in his seat. I hadn't seen him for a while, and he couldn't believe how grown-up Jared and I were. I looked at the auditorium entrance anxiously every second to see if my father would walk in proudly with his blazer and slick haircut.

Dad never walked through that door, though, which made me sad. *How could he miss my mother's proudest moment?* Was he ashamed to see her family, or did he just not care? This carried with me as I went from happy to sad, back and forth, like a rollercoaster of emotions, throughout the whole ceremony. I hugged my mother so tightly after the ceremony was over; if Dad wasn't there for her, then at least I would be—always. *She will never lose me,* I thought as I squeezed her tighter.

The following weekend, Jared and I visited our father. I didn't even want to mention Mom's ceremony and how he had missed it last week; it would upset me too much. He told us that he had gone on a date with another woman. My face flushed as I started to sweat. *How could he move on so quickly and forget about Mom?* I thought about how one day, if he decided to remarry, I would have another woman in my life. *I need to get away from this,* I thought as I closed my eyes and fell asleep.

This would officially be the first Christmas that Jared and I would sleep until noon on Christmas Day. I mean, what was the point of waking up if our family was broken? There would be no more days of my mom and dad sitting tiredly by the Christmas tree, watching us open presents before my mother made coffee for my father and breakfast for us. No more of my dad guessing what was under the wrapping and always getting it right. The holiday was depressing now.

○ ○ ○

I was looking forward to getting my learner's permit soon; finally, I would have some freedom from all of this nonsense. My mother had found a career as an LPN at a senior living home for elderly patients. I'm not sure why, but she loved helping people; she was the sweetest woman in the world. Every time I was down, she knew exactly what to say to make me smile again. She had a career now, so there would be no more selling cosmetics; she could support her two sons without a husband.

At one point, however, my father told us we were going to have to sell the house, and when we did, my mother would need to find an apartment, but that it was going to take a little bit of time. My mother and father also told me that I would need a job if I was going to have a car and would be buying gas to run it.

Over the next several weeks, I applied for basic job positions so I would have a little cash while I had my driving classes that started soon. I filled out applications to supermarkets, landscape companies, anything, really. I didn't care what I was doing, I just needed to have cash to have freedom to drive.

My first real job was at the supermarket down the street. It was convenient because I could walk there after school and work for a couple of hours, which ended up being about twenty to thirty hours per week. Just enough money to take home two hundred dollars a week, which would be enough for gas money and spending money. The job was boring and simple; I was a bagger, which consisted of putting items in bags for customers. While doing that, I was also taking driving classes a couple of nights a week. Sometimes I would see my basketball friends' parents at the store. I would smile and put their food in paper or plastic for them. Their kids, my friends, didn't need jobs, since they were all wealthy and already had nice cars lined up for them, which I resented. Everyone told me that working builds character, but I always thought that was just what people said who already had money.

My baseball tryouts had started after basketball came to an end. It was time for "Catfish" to shine. Mr. Hillfield was at tryouts, talking to the varsity coach, bragging how perfect I was, as they watched me pitch strike after strike. He smiled at me like I was his golden boy, but I wondered if he knew that his golden boy was struggling in his personal life.

The varsity coach came over and talked with me about how they wanted to keep me as a backup pitcher and possibly bring me up to the team, but that they already had a lot of seniors who were strong pitchers. He said that he would keep an eye on me and watch how I pitched this season for Mr. Hillfield.

I was excited to hear that I was still going to be a starter for my baseball team, at least. Most of my teammates were kids I had played with last year, and we had a solid-looking team. The only difference between this year and last was that my family would not be at all of my games, so I had no support. My mom was working all the time, and sometimes through the night. Day shifts ran into night shifts, and sometimes Jared and I didn't see Mom for a couple of days. It seemed like she was always either working or sleeping.

My mother never got to see how good her son was at baseball anymore, which kind of made me sad. My father would attend as many games as he could, but most of the time I would walk to my games in my uniform, alone. I think that I was good at pitching because when I was on the mound, it was just me. I would put my emotions and all of my problems into the baseball and throw it as hard as I could, channeling all of my hate and anger toward the world. I could be completely focused, and I blocked out both the crowd and the world when I was on the mound. I hoped that one day I could be a college pitcher, and that my mother and father would get back together to watch their son play.

I continued to hang out with Rory and Tyler, and they also introduced me to a couple other friends, Jake and Mark. I had my baseball friends who were all about sports, and then I had my other friends who mainly smoked weed, drank, and skipped classes. I was stuck in the middle way; I still wasn't into the whole party scene and never felt tempted by booze or weed, but I liked some of the kids who were.

My grades had started to slip a bit because I was also working at the supermarket and finishing up my driving classes. Whenever I had free time, I would walk over to Rory's to hang out with the guys. I would say I was about a C student at this point, compared to the honor-roll student I had been.

◉ ◉ ◉

The day had arrived; my mother drove me to the RMV. I was as nervous as could be to take my road test. This meant so much to me—I needed to pass the test and get my license: the freedom was too important to lose. I had been practicing for weeks and had become a pretty confident driver. The test consisted of a cop and me sitting in the front seat, while my mother waited in her car. The cop held his clipboard and took notes as I tightened my seatbelt and adjusted my mirrors. I slowly backed the car out of the parking spot and could feel my heart racing as I saw my mother watching in the background. I steered the car down the street as I cautiously signaled my blinker on and then came to a full stop at an intersection. We arrived at a side street and I parallel-parked; the policeman then had me finish the rest of the drive back to the RMV.

"Congratulations, Mr. Michaels," he said as he handed me my passed application so that I could get my temporary license. I smiled and acted confident as my mother thanked the officer.

"That was it?" I said. It felt as though he had barely tested me, but I had passed with flying colors. Freedom was here, and now I just needed a car.

I felt like a new man when we pulled into the driveway. Then, I noticed it. In the driveway, there was a silver and gold Chevy pickup truck. It had tinted windows and huge tires. As we pulled in the driveway slowly, my mom and I looked in the truck's window to see a familiar figure. As we parked, the truck door opened.

"What's up, dude?" My father walked over to my mother and me, and told us that this was his new truck. He had me hop in and burn rubber down the street after he congratulated me. It was like he was a teenager again; he looked happy as we raced down the street, causing the neighbors to yell. He laughed as he looked over to me and tossed me a key; I looked down at the key and saw a Dodge symbol.

"It's all yours," he said.

"No way, really?" I couldn't help but smile. Ecstasy rushed through my body as we pulled into his apartment complex to see my new car—his old Dodge. I was the proud owner of a maroon '89 Dodge Caravan with over 130,000 miles on it. I mean, it was no new car like my friends had, but at least now I wouldn't have to walk to baseball and to school; I had my freedom, finally. He told me that as long as I keep a job, it was mine.

"Deal," I said.

My world suddenly felt easier; every time I felt down, I could get in my car and drive away. Of course, because I had just gotten my license, I had to follow the curfew for new drivers. I couldn't have anyone in the car after eleven.

I left my house and immediately drove to Rory's, where he and Tyler were sitting in the backyard, smoking cigarettes, laughing, and having a good time.

"Hop in, guys," I said as I pulled up, excited.

"No way; this thing's awesome," they replied. They put their cigarettes out and jumped in as we cruised the town, free as birds. After we drove around for what must have been five hours straight, taking the car to the beach and all around town, I dropped them off and had to go to work. Stop & Shop was boring me, and now that I had a car, I wanted a new job. I was sick of seeing all of my sports buddies' parents judging me while I bagged their groceries.

On the weekends, I started to apply for jobs at local businesses, landscaping companies, and anything that seemed better than the supermarket. Ironically, I found a job at Butcher Boy Markets, a family-owned company that served high quality meats and foods. I landed a quiet job in the Bakery Department, where I worked with five other people. The pay was a little better and my job would mainly be to serve pastries, package bread, make bread crumbs, and make sure we always had fresh pastries. It was pretty easy and I didn't really have to work too hard; I just wanted a paycheck so that I could have spending money.

Later that night, I arrived home excited to surprise my mother with the good news. She was working the night shift again, though. Jared said that my dad was going to pick us up to have dinner at his place. I figured that we could just drive over instead. Jared and I got to his house and found that the place was a mess. We watched TV in the living room and he cooked dinner for us, but during the hour his cell phone must have rung twenty-five times before he finally turned it off. I wasn't sure what was going on, but I could tell that he was furious.

The next day, my mother was in her bedroom as I slowly walked in to see her crying and wiping her eyes. She was a very honest woman and never kept secrets from her sons and told me that my father had not only cheated on her, but also that the woman had been her best friend. Besides that, Dad had been with multiple other women who were mothers of kids on my brother's hockey team. It crushed my soul to hear this, and I went into a state of panic. All I could feel was hate running through my body. Her tears grew larger as she headed off to bed; I didn't know how to cope with this emotionally draining shocker.

Normally, I would go over to the school and shoot hoops, but this time, the pain ran deeper as I burned out of my driveway in my van to drive to Rory's house. *He would understand*, I thought. *His parents went through the same thing.* I couldn't run to any of my buddies on the baseball or basketball team, because they wouldn't get it. Rory and Tyler were there in the backyard; it seemed like they never left those Adirondack chairs. I pulled up a chair and asked for a cigarette as I sighed.

"What's wrong, man?" they asked.

"Just my parents; I found out my dad had been cheating on my mom for a while now, and she was crying in bed."

They seemed genuinely understanding. Tyler lit up a joint, and I smelled it burning from the corner of my nose. "Let me have a hit," I said. *Screw it; could things get any worse?*

As I inhaled, my head got light and my throat burned up with smoke; I coughed for a minute straight. "Holy shit," I said as my eyes got heavy and my body felt like it had sunk into a shell. My heart raced fast and then slowed down. I laughed for no reason.

"Good, right?" Rory laughed, and then Tyler laughed and I laughed. All I could think about was Rory at the basketball court telling me that one day I would smoke. *Did he plan this?* My mind raced, almost as if I had figured out the whole world in the blink of an eye, and then *POOF!* I forgot what I was thinking about and continued to laugh. My eyelids got heavier as I began to forget my problems and became officially as high as a kite.

Later, I cranked up the music and lit a cigarette as I drove home. My house was only two blocks from Rory's, but it was the longest ride of my life. I walked into the house and found that everyone was asleep. I headed into the kitchen, aggressively rumbling through the cabinets for any food. I grabbed a package of Oreos and turned on the TV, eating nonstop. I could hear myself chewing and laughed. After eating all the Oreos, I passed out on the couch. *This is a new life for me,* I thought, *I love being high.*

BEEP! BEEP! My alarm clock rang loudly as I woke up for school. My mother was scheduled for a double shift and had left for work already, and my brother had walked to school. I hit the snooze button and went back to bed. I didn't want to deal with school; I was sick of wearing a fake smile for everyone. My teammates didn't understand, and neither did my teachers; girls were annoying and too often played mind games with me. I just wanted to go back to sleep.

Once I woke up later that day, I drove to my baseball game. I wasn't pitching this game and was instead resting my arm on the bench. I saw Rory and Tyler sitting by the bleachers, calling my name. After the game ended, I said goodbye to everyone quickly while Tyler and Rory and I hopped in my van. Tyler pulled out a joint and I smiled, saying, "Nice, spark it up," as I took off my baseball hat.

Tyler lit up the joint as I drove down some back streets. It was my first "joint cruise," he called it, as we laughed and turned up the music. I inhaled the first hit and there it was, unfolding right there in my car—the feeling of life getting easier. My mind raced with thoughts and I couldn't stop snickering. We must have laughed for an hour straight, and I honestly had no clue why I had been laughing in the first place. We went to Rory's house afterward, where I introduced myself to his mom, who didn't even care that we were all stoned. We grabbed some chips and went up to his room to listen to music; I sat back on his futon and we chilled for hours.

That night, my mother was waiting in the kitchen as I walked through the door quietly. Her look felt almost as though she was looking directly into my soul, like she knew that something was up. I quickly walked past her and went into my room, wondering if she knew. She knocked on my door and asked if I was okay.

"Yeah, just tired from my game, I'm going to bed."

School the next day was a blur; I didn't want to be there, but the year was almost ending. Though my baseball buddies started to notice, they didn't say much about me hanging out more with Tyler and Rory. I would smoke pot with those guys almost every day.

Summer was approaching and I couldn't wait. Finally baseball would be over, school would be over, and I had my license. My brother and I continued to visit my father a couple of nights a week, and he continued to get strange calls from blocked numbers. He was constantly frustrated, and I still didn't know what was going on. I didn't even care anymore; I would just get high and try to ignore the situation.

Jared and I stopped talking; he was turning thirteen soon and had no older brother supporting him. I wasn't there to help with any advice, and never looked at life from his perspective; I could barely handle my own life. I started to sweep all my problems under the rug and avoid them.

CHAPTER 6

LOST AND NOT KNOWING

F inal exams finished up for my sophomore year. I had passed all of my courses and would be moving on to become a junior. The past month had been hard on my family, especially after finding out my father's secret. Her name was Gloria, and she was a lot younger than he was; she must have been in her late twenties or early thirties. She was a friend of one of my father's sisters who had set them up on a blind date. The fact that my father was seeing another woman made me sick to my stomach, and I would get high to dull the pain. Gloria was the reason behind my father's phone ringing back to back, and the voicemails after every call. He had been intimate with her, my mother told me, and I was convinced that she was crazy.

I know that most people would think that I was jumping to conclusions, that she was not crazy, but in fact she was literally, clinically crazy. She had been a patient in mental institutions on multiple occasions, she was unemployed, and she would stalk my father from a different car almost every week. Apparently, my father never knew that she was insane; however, his life was becoming difficult because she started to bring our family into the picture.

Gloria had threatened my mom, saying she would kill her. My heart beat rapidly like a drum when my mother told me this. *Who the hell is this lady to talk negatively about my mother? She doesn't even know her. Great way to start the summer.* I rolled my eyes. *At least Rory is having a party at his house tonight,* I thought.

Rory had invited everyone that he could think of; his mother was out of town and he had the place to himself. His house wasn't big, but his yard had plenty of space. The night was beautiful, so I threw on my summer shorts and polo shirt and jumped into my van. I drove over to Rory's and saw a lot of familiar faces from school, including many pretty girls. *What more could we ask for at sixteen?* Joints were being passed around; I took hits and laughed. While I was in the middle of telling one of my stories, a girl tapped on my shoulder. I had never seen her before; she had blondish-reddish hair and a pale complexion. She wasn't really my type, but she was friendly and poured me a shot of Goldschläger. It had gold crystals floating in it which, she said, was real gold. I played it off cool as if I drank alcohol all of the time.

She poured the first shot as my heart raced, but I kept mellow from the marijuana. *I had never even had a beer before, should I drink this?* I thought of Gloria and said, "Fuck it," as I downed the first shot. *AHHH!* As the blood rushed to my face, turning it red, I felt like I had jumped out of an airplane. Where had alcohol been my whole life? My inhibitions vanished as I matched her on another shot. By the time the third shot was over, this red-headed blonde girl started to become more attractive and funny. The whole party crowd huddled around me: I had just taken three shots within five minutes. My confidence grew as I downed another Goldschläger shot and lit up a cigarette.

"What's up now? You can't beat me," I said confidently. I had fallen in love with the feeling of drunkenness. I didn't care what would happen tomorrow, I didn't care how much my life had changed over the past few months; all that mattered was living in the moment. "Logan, Logan, Logan!"

"No more for me," she said, as I stood up, wobbly. Rory began to look blurry as he laughed at me; I slurred my words to him and stumbled out of the kitchen and into the backyard. He followed me out as I lit up a cigarette and fell over backwards onto his Adirondack chair.

"Dude, you just took ten shots in one hour!"

"Is that bad?" I replied. I told Rory not to worry as I walked over to his mom's garden and started to piss on the flowers while smoking my cigarette. Tyler came over to help me after I fell into the garden.

"Logan, let's get you home," he said, as my peers came outside to watch me humiliate myself. Mark, a sober guy at the party, took me home to my mom's house; I cursed him out from the backseat the whole time. Once the car stopped, I immediately ran out and fell on my face. Mark carried me to my mother's front door; she had just gotten home from work. I slightly remember that my mother was near tears as she asked Mark if I was on drugs.

He said, "No, Mrs. Michaels—he just drank way too much." I slammed the door shut in his face.

The next morning I woke up alone, and in my mother's bed. As I opened my eyes, I realized that I was still drunk. Then I realized that not only had I fallen asleep in my mother's bed, but that I had also pissed in it. She came into the room looking very concerned.

"I shouldn't have drank that much, Mom," I said when I

stumbled out of bed at noon. I couldn't bear for my mother to see me hung over, so I walked to Rory's house; I couldn't even drive because I felt lost. I felt like days had passed and the whole world was in slow motion. I finally arrived at Rory's, sweating profusely from the alcohol, and I saw Tyler and Rory getting high and laughing as I walked up.

"You're the man, dude. How do you like drinking?"

"It's awesome," I replied, "Besides today." I took a hit of the joint, which made me feel better.

I had summer league basketball the next day, but decided to skip it after the previous night. I also figured that I would call in sick to work because, technically, I *was* sick. Instead, Rory, Tyler, and I walked back to my house to get my van. My mother had gone to work and Jared was home watching TV. It was the first time that my friends met Jared, and he seemed lost and confused. He didn't say much as I left him to go for a cruise in the van. I was so caught up in my insecurities that I let the poor kid sit there, all alone. At the time though, getting high was my priority, and it took my pain away. Before I could help to take away my family's pain, I needed to deal with my own.

We cruised through North Andover, "fish bowling" my car. That's basically when you leave the windows up and smoke marijuana inside. By the time the joint was done, I had no clue where I was. Sometimes, we would get so high that we would drive for hours aimlessly and usually end up getting McDonald's or Burger King. After every joint or bowl we smoked, I loved smoking a cigarette. I could see the chemicals burning slowly on the cigarette and dissolving the paper; it was pretty trippy. Plus, I had officially bought my first pack of Marlboro Reds. What had started off as a here-and-there habit was now an everyday routine. I needed them.

After driving for hours, we finally got back to Rory's house. Tyler's older brother, Greg, walked over. He was laidback and into pills and heavier drugs. I stayed far away from that. He had a couple of older friends who would buy us alcohol, so I decided to get a twelve-pack of Budweiser.

"I'll stay away from the hard liquor tonight," I said.

We sat in the Adirondack chairs for hours drinking beers, smoking joints, and laughing all night. It felt good to just chill with the guys. I started to forget about all of my other friends; I couldn't relate to them anymore. I became more mellowed after drinking eight beers—I guess, for someone who had just started to drink, I had a pretty high tolerance. Because I was drunk, I decided to walk home through the baseball field. Normally, I was creeped out by walking through the schoolyard; I always imagined that someone was following me, as I walked, feeling paranoid. However, the buzz from the beer made me confident enough to walk home.

My mother would be working a double-shift until the next morning. The house seemed quiet, and I soon passed out on my bed. I woke up in a panic during the middle of the night; for some reason, I had a feeling that something was wrong. I could feel the wind blowing up the stairs, and the smell of summer creeping up the stairs. I thought I could hear voices, but I was too tired to move, so I lay back down.

Morning arrived and I wasn't sure whether last night had been a dream or reality. Every time I smoked, I would have such vivid dreams, and it was almost as it was another life was calling me and pulling me away from this life. I could never figure it out, and just when I would feel like I had the whole world solved, my mind would go blank. I guess it was the effects of marijuana.

"It smells like paint," I said to my mom as I woke up. She ran over to the front door to see that it was slightly open, as if it had never been fully shut. I could have sworn that I'd shut it, and so had my mom. After we both started into the kitchen, we heard a *BANG! BANG!* Approaching the front door cautiously, my mother saw two police officers standing there.

"Is Jared Michaels home?" they asked.

"Yes, officer, he should be in his room."

"May we come in?"

Jared came out of his room, and his big, dark eyes looked nervous. "May we see your shoes, Jared?" the officers asked. I looked over at Jared's shoes to see streaks of paint on them. *No wonder it smelled like paint. Wait, was that a dream I was having last night—or was it Jared?*

Jared put his head down and looked at my mother and me as though he knew he was busted. Last night's noise had not been the wind gusting, and it hadn't been the summer breeze. My twelve-year-old brother, whom I had left alone that night, was arrested for vandalism. He had taken spray paint from our basement, and with a couple of his friends had vandalized the elementary school with large pictures of penises and swear words. The officers handcuffed him as they put him in the back of the cop car.

"What an idiot," I said out loud. "What the hell was he thinking, Mom?"

I was almost in complete denial that this was happening; how could my brother have been so stupid to do something like *this*? He had held in everything that was happening to him, but, clearly, he was not okay.

My mother and I arrived at the district court in Lawrence where Jared was held in jail for a couple of nights. Those may have been the longest three nights I had ever experienced, and all I could think about was jail scenes in movies and whether my brother was getting beat up. What had happened to my carefree brother at the Cape, throwing the football on the beach and smiling with our whole family? My eyes would water and fill with tears, but I never cried; I held my emotions in for as long as I could.

My mother had hired a family lawyer, someone her brother

knew, to represent Jared. I sat in the back of the courtroom with my mother. I remember looking around at all of the young criminals in the courtroom who had no cares in the world. I turned my hat backwards as the judge called the court case for "Jared Michaels." My baby brother came out in handcuffs with the court officer, who sat him in front of the judge. My mother looked worried, fearful that this incident would ruin Jared's life. Since he was a minor, he was put on probation until the age of eighteen, and he had to do community service until he was fifteen. The judge had made my brother seem like a thug. I sighed loudly and cursed under my breath. The judge heard me and kicked me out of the courtroom. I had so much anger during that moment. My brother wasn't a bad kid; he just had no guidance, and I blamed myself for that.

After the awful nightmare of being in court, I called Rory immediately to get some weed. He had a contact who sold pounds of weed and would sell small bags for forty bucks. This would be the first bag of weed that I bought on my own. Rory and I went over to his house, where he had bongs and pounds of weed on the table; I had never seen that much before. He bagged up an ounce of weed and we smoked out of his gravity bong. After the first hit I took, I thought I was going to die; I coughed for ten minutes. We must have stayed at his house for hours, smoking. Looking in the mirror, I saw a different person. I was broken, my dreams were crushed, my family had been ripped apart, and my brother was completely lost. The only thing that would take my pain away was getting high.

Once we left, the drive home was a nightmare; I was so high that I couldn't even remember driving. *WOOP! WOOP!*

"What the hell is that, Rory?" The blue lights flashed behind me as my heart started to shake out of my body, and my mouth became even drier than it was already. *The cops are behind us, fuck!* I had never been pulled over before and I had weed on me. What the hell would my mother do if I got arrested a couple days after Jared? it would kill her. I tucked the bag of weed into my sock as I strapped my seatbelt on.

"License and registration," the cop said, as I became paranoid because my eyes were completely bloodshot.

"Here you go, officer," I said confidently. *I can't be caught,* I reminded myself. The policeman sat in his car behind me for about ten minutes, and I felt like he was waiting to search the car. He came back, handed me my license, and asked if I was related to Jared Michaels. My blood pressure rose in my face as I said, "Yes; he is my brother." In my head, something clicked because my fear disappeared.

He then said, "Okay, well, I am going to keep an eye on you; get out of here." I drove away relieved but furious, because he had immediately judged me. How can someone who doesn't even know you judge you so quickly? I went to bed that night angry. My day had felt so long, and it felt too long before I was finally able to shut my bloodshot eyes.

The next day, I woke up early and drove over to Rory's; we rolled a joint and got high. Tyler came over to match us on another joint. We talked about how much we hated the cops. Rory said that his mother was gone for the weekend again, so we got our cell phones out and started to call some girls to persuade them to come party at his house tonight. We smoked weed all day, ate fast food, and then went for bowl cruises. I must have been smoking half a pack of cigarettes a day. I remember that it had started with just smoking one, here and there, but now I was addicted to them. We knew a local buddy at the convenience store who would sell us packs anytime we wanted.

After rounding up some high school girls, we got the alcohol and started the party. I drank beers and took shots until I had no remorse. My hands would wander as I grabbed girls' butts with no care, as we sparked up joints and watched the girls stripping to music.

This was the life I wanted to live, I thought.

Tyler, Rory and I were becoming best friends. This very night, when I was so high and drunk, was when Michelle from across the street grabbed my hand and brought me upstairs. Even though I was drunk, I was still nervous—I was a virgin, and I knew that she had had sex before.

We started to make out and I could taste the beer on her breath; I'm sure she also tasted it on mine. We were both breathing so heavily while rubbing each other's body. She slowly started moving her hand down my pants as I became harder and harder. I rubbed her as I started to take her shirt off, and began to suck on her nipples. She pulled my penis out and started to stroke it as she moaned from me stroking her. We were both naked minutes later on Rory's parents' bed. I stopped her. "Wait, I need a condom."

I ran over to Rory's room, banging on the door, and when he opened it up, I could see he had a girl in there, too. He gave me a condom and I ran back into the room. Michelle pushed me onto the bed and put the condom on me, then jumped onto me and started to ride me. She thrust back and forth as she moaned and grabbed onto my chest and scratched me aggressively. It may have lasted only five minutes, but it seemed like an hour. I finished and was no longer a virgin; this was not my dream girl, but with the amount of alcohol and weed I had smoked, she looked the best that night.

● ◉ ◉

Morning arrived as I woke up in Rory's parents' bed. I had no clue where I was for a second, and then I realized I was naked. I went downstairs and saw Tyler and Rory watching TV while smoking a joint. They smirked as I came down with my hair a mess, looking hung over. "What a great night," I said, laughing.

This was by far the best summer I had ever had, and I started to forget about Cape Cod.

Later, I went home to get some rest and saw my mother. She looked sad to see her two sons drifting apart. I didn't come home much anymore. I would either be working at Butcher Boy or smoking and drinking at Rory's house. I found out that Jared was starting his probation at the community center, where my basketball team played. The whole high school and all of my basketball buddies would see Jared picking up trash outside by the courts. It disgusted me that they would see my brother and judge him.

My first summer league basketball game was the next day. I dropped Jared off for his community service and opened my door because my game was at the same time. As I saw Jared walking in, I paused, and shut my door. *Fuck this,* I thought. I turned my car back on and called Rory. "I'm skipping summer league; let's get high." My cell phone began to ring immediately as I drove off. "Stop calling me," I said under my breath. My team had seen me driving away in my red van. I shut off my phone; I didn't feel like explaining why I was leaving. *Who would understand?*

We got stoned for hours until we all passed out. When I woke up, I realized that I had forgotten to pick up my brother. I drove to the house and ran in to see him by himself playing video games on the couch.

"How the hell did you get home?"

"I walked," he replied.

"No way," I said. "It must have been two miles, sorry."

With a "whatever," he continued to play video games. I realized right there how crappy of an older brother I had become. He and I used to do everything together; he was my best friend, not just my brother. My mother was working a double-shift again, and I walked upstairs feeling depressed after realizing how shitty a person I had become. I just wanted to go to bed and never wake up. Or maybe I would wake up and this would all be a dream: my parents would be together, Jared wouldn't be on probation, and I would be a perfect older brother like I had always imagined.

In the following couple of days, my brother, father, and I had dinner together. We went over to Dad's apartment down the street and he didn't mention one word about Jared's probation. It was kind of a relief not to talk about it, and I think he understood. He told stories of how he would get in trouble all the time and tried to shed some laughter on the situation. We all laughed about life, and he actually made things seem not so bad. His phone would continue to ring, and he ignored it while we were eating dinner. He finally opened up later that night after he drank a couple of beers.

"This woman is crazy; if any weird woman approaches you, stay away from her. She knows about your mother and is after her. She thinks we are still together and wants her out of the picture, so protect your mother."

"Do terrible things just all happen at once?" I asked. "This is a nightmare, why would you even get involved with this woman?" My dad got angry as he blew my question off, just saying that he didn't know.

"Thanks for dinner," I replied sarcastically and left. He called my name, but let me go; we were supposed to sleep at his house that night, so Jared stayed, but I drove to Rory's house instead.

"Let's get high," I said.

"We need to get some first," Rory replied. We drove over to his dealer's house and hung out for a little bit.

Buying weed was almost a regular event now, and the dealer and I grew pretty close; he was a cool kid, and only a year older than us. We smoked all night, and even had a couple of beers at his house. Rory and I left after getting a nice buzz, and went for a cruise. It was the first time I had ever driven drunk; *it's not that bad,* I thought.

The next day, my mother had the whole day off and could relax. I felt like the three of us, she, Jared and I, hadn't been together in a long, long time. We watched TV and laughed together; it was nice to see her happy again, or at least for the moment. She had her two sons together, which always brought a smile to her face. Even though Jared was on probation, she still treated him like the little boy he was. She was a single mother with a career now, but she always made sure we had a warm, cooked meal and a roof over our heads. *She is one of the strongest people I can imagine,* I thought.

Later that evening, a car pulled up in front of our house. A man wearing a cable company hat and uniform approached the door and banged on it a couple of times. My mother went over to the door and saw a man who looked shady; he had awful yellow teeth, his eyes were bugged out, and his uniform was untucked and sloppy.

"Maria Michaels? I am here to fix a cable issue." My mother backed away from the door and locked it quickly, as he tried to open it and come inside. Jared and I ran over to the door as he ran back to his car and drove off.

"That man wasn't with the cable company, Mom. He was trying to hurt you; it must have been the woman Dad's been with."

My mom was frightened as she locked the doors and windows. She then called the cable company to confirm this and they said that there had been had no appointment for her at all. I wanted this Gloria dead. *I would die for my mother,* I thought, *and kill whoever tried to hurt her.* It made me angry to the point where I wanted to chase down this creep. My mother told me to relax; she didn't want me doing anything. We called the cops and made them at least aware of the situation, but they didn't do much to help.

My mother had to work that night, and I don't know how she kept her composure together or where she got her strength.

I knew that she had had a hard home life from all that she'd told me and Jared, but was not sure what other things had happened in her past. Having my own car helped me let go of things, and I would sometimes drive aimlessly for hours, listening to music and thinking about life. I was always a heavy thinker, but ever since I started smoking pot, I noticed that my depression had grown. It was a hard feeling to shake.

Most of all of my days were sad, and I didn't have too many days where I was okay anymore. The only thing alcohol and weed did for me was postpone my sadness, but once I sobered up, I was back to reality: I was not happy. I was miserable with my life. I started to wonder if I had ever been happy, or at least tried to remember happy times in my past.

⊙ ⊙ ⊙

Summer had been flying past and was almost over. I had pretty much quit summer league basketball. I would make up excuses every time I had a game: I was on vacation, I was sick, or I just wouldn't pick up the phone.

One humid summer night, Rory, Tyler, two girls in the grade above us and I took a cruise. I had bought a large beanbag in the back of my van so that the girls could sit on it. We drove around town aimlessly, smoking joints and cigarettes, passing bottles of vodka, and having a blast. I'm not sure how life started to change for me so quickly, but I was finally having fun. I guess substituting anything real with drugs and alcohol made me forget about my parents' divorce. So that summer, my group had expanded to include Rita and Kristen. They were the two year-older wild girls who were down for anything. They would actually call us to pick them up so that we all could drink and drive around. Summer nights were coming home with a nice buzz to the smell of fresh air, and raiding the kitchen cabinets and fridge to warm up a Hot Pocket® or to eat an entire bag of chips. This was my new Cape Cod. I didn't want this summer to end, but junior year was fast approaching and I hadn't played basketball once in the past couple of months. To be honest, I didn't care what happened with sports anymore.

"Logan! Wake up," my mother yelled. *UGH!*

"Ma, just let me stay home today."

"It's the first day of school; there's no way you're staying home." I was so tired from my marijuana habits, especially since I would smoke almost every day, and if I hadn't smoked it was only because I couldn't find anyone with weed. My mother drove off to work after she woke me; she was scheduled for the morning shift. Jared walked to middle school with a friend and I jumped into my van to pick up Rory and Tyler. Surprisingly, they were held back a couple years in a row and would be seniors this year. As I turned the corner on my first day back, I saw the jocks sitting together in a group with their Abercrombie sweaters and turtlenecks—it made me sick. They all had on perfect smiles, and they were laughing and joking about their perfect fucking summers.

I'm not sure why I was so mad; if I wanted, I could have gone over to them and sat down to talk about basketball tryouts in a couple weeks. However, as I started to approach them, I came to complete halt halfway there. Trying to smile and pretend that things in my life were perfect was just not happening today.

"Let's go, guys," I said. Tyler, Rory, and I ran down the hall as the bell rang. While I sped down the hallway, I saw Tim from basketball. We locked eyes for a minute as I passed him. He knew that I had been hanging with the "wrong crowd" and looked away as I ran out the door and into the parking lot. We turned the corner to run to my van and jumped in. I turned on the ignition and pulled out just as a car swerved in front of me, bringing us to a complete stop. A man wearing a police uniform got out.

"Out of the car, boys," he said, "Where are you heading? Isn't class is about to start?"

"We were just running back to my house; I forgot some notes for class," Rory said.

"Bullshit," the officer replied. "Get into class."

He made me park, took down our names, and watched us walk to class. I felt like an idiot as I walked into class, late, with everyone staring at me. Especially since I hadn't seen anyone all summer. I slouched down in my chair and threw my hoodie over my head like a thug who had no care for school. Class ended after an hour and then I felt someone tap on my shoulder.

"What's up with you?" Tim asked.

"Nothing; I'm fine," I said as I brushed away from him. Tim asked if I was trying out for the team as I walked away to find Tyler and Rory. I turned and said, "Yeah man, I'll be there."

"Logan! Let's get out of here." I saw Tyler, Rory, and Jake, a new kid that started to hang out with us more often. Jake was another product of a broken home. We all ran to the exit door, looking for the school cop. He was nowhere to be found, so we ran out to my van again and hopped in.

"Shit, there he is, coming from the other side of the school," Rory said as I turned on the ignition and burnt out of the parking lot. Rory's head flew back as I peeled out of the lot. "GO! GO! GO!" I floored it; we sped up the side streets and as we turned onto street after street, I could feel the cop getting closer. He never showed up, though, and we approached my house.

My mother was working until three and Jared was at school. Now we had the house to ourselves, so we lit up a joint on the porch and laughed while smoking it.

"I can't believe we just ran from the cops," we laughed.

No one noticed four kids smoking weed on a porch, so it was perfect. I had skipped my first day of junior year and didn't have a care in the world; I would just say I was sick, and my mother would never know. At three o'clock I ditched my job and we would just leave and go to Rory's house and chill outside in his Adirondack chairs.

As we approached the back of his yard, laughing and passing around a joint, we heard a siren come up behind us. Rory threw the joint under an old broken-down car in his yard.

"Are you fucking kidding me?" Tyler yelled. Officer Pinelli had tracked down where we all lived and had shown up at Rory's house. Pinelli accused us of skipping school, but unfortunately for him, we all played it cool and said we had been there and were just getting home. It was perfect timing, and he had no proof, let alone no evidence of marijuana, even though our eyes were completely bloodshot.

"I'm going to be watching you all," he threatened as he pulled away. We just laughed afterward and walked into the house.

That night, my mother got home and as soon as the door slammed shut, she came at me faster than a speeding bullet.

"Logan, school called and said you weren't there."

"Well, I was," I replied, but couldn't look her in the eyes.

"What's going on with you?" she asked.

"Screw you, Mom!"

"Excuse me?" she replied, wide-eyed. That was the first time I had ever cursed at my mom and it felt awful, but I resented her for accusing me. Jared watched me slam the door to my room, and he stared after at me with his confused adolescent eyes. I think that at this point we all knew things were officially going downhill.

School sucked, and even though basketball tryouts were coming up in a couple weeks, I didn't even want to try out. I decided that I'd rather smoke weed and chill with my buddies. *Fuck school,* I thought. Besides, all of the richie-rich kids would judge me anyway, especially since I'd been skipping school a couple times a week. It had started when we skipped the first day and ran from Officer Pinelli.

I continued to cut class and had gotten detentions and tardies, and had been forced into multiple appointments with my guidance counselor. Mr. Nedrow was my guidance counselor; he must have been thirty five years old, but looked twenty five. All of the high school girls loved him. He would ask me how I felt about my parents being divorced and about what had happened to my brother.

"Shit happens," I told him, "What can I do? I'm fine."

What was I supposed to tell him? That my fucking world was falling apart, that my brother wouldn't even speak to me, that I had no relationship with my dad, and that my mother and I were slowly distancing? *Screw that.* What would that accomplish, and did he really care or was he just setting me up so that he could fill out his fucking perfect report?

My crowd of punks grew bigger the more that I skipped school. We had a crew of about ten guys who would sneak out of class, one by one, throughout the day. Rory's mother got sick, so we started to party at my house during the school hours.

A typical day in my junior year was waking up and waiting for my mom to go to work and then either going back to bed or driving over to Rory's and taking bong rips in the morning. I think I was officially a loser, since I never went to classes and, when I did, I only did enough to cheat on tests in order to barely pass. The first semester was almost over and the only class I was passing was Mr. Hillfield's class, and even he knew something was up with me. I would slouch back in class with a black hoodie over my head. When the teachers would call my name, I'd ignore them until they kicked me out of class. Everyone knew I was slipping, but I didn't want to listen.

◉ ◎ ◎

Basketball tryouts that year were interesting. My heart was beating out of my chest as if the drummer boy was in there. The cigarettes made my lungs feel filled up after just a couple times down the court. Since my lungs felt collapsed, I could barely hit the jump shots that I used to hit easily. Younger and older kids were whizzing right by me; I was not "Ice" anymore. The coach looked at me like I was a completely different person, and I didn't want to hear it. I didn't make varsity like I had always imagined; I was stuck on the bench for the JV team—as an upperclassman. Not long ago, the whole world had been calling my name, and my dream girl had been so close, but now I smoked weed until my eyes turned red and I couldn't even run up the court. *What the hell has happened to Logan?*

Some nights, when my mother wasn't working, I would come home and walk by her door on my way upstairs. I could hear a whimpering cry as I walked past. My heart told me to stop what I was doing and hug her, but my adolescent mind continued up the stairs and ignored it. My father had told me that her family had been dirt poor and that her father's sickness had started when she was young.

"I always wanted to make her rich and take her pain away, but that dream started to fade away, as I was only making things harder on her."

⊙ ⊙ ⊙

Butcher Boy was awful, and once again, I walked into the store high and ready to package bread crumbs. The girls who worked there were so hot, though. Looking through the glass bread case that day was this amazing girl. She must have been my age, or maybe she was closer to seventeen. For months, she would peek at me through the glass. I finally ran into her taking the trash out in the back. Her name was Tiffany, and she had a tough Boston accent. I was shy, but managed to say hello; she smiled and said hello back.

"We should hang out sometime," I said.

"Sure," she said as she wrote her phone number on my hand. I figured that I could have her come over to my house for a party sometime. In a couple of nights, my brother would be over my dad's and my mother would be working a double-shift at the nursing home all night.

I texted Tiffany to invite her to my house party, and had Rory text all the people he knew. The party was a mix of jocks and burnouts and cute girls. We had some freshman girls that Rory knew come over. They were so quiet and shy, but we had enough liquor for the whole party and weed to pass around. Tiffany showed up after the third shot of vodka went down my throat.

"Hey baby," I yelled as I ran over, hugged her aggressively, and squeezed her butt. She loved it, I assumed, since she laughed and took a shot. My house was filled with probably about twenty people, all underage drinking; girls and guys were hooking up on the couch, and Rory was in my mother's room with some girl. The party was awesome, and everyone was just having a good time.

Tiffany and I went upstairs to my room as I found myself hammered. I mean, I could barely see anything at this point. Every time I would drink, it wasn't even about having fun—I would get blackout drunk.

Tiffany jumped on top of me, but I was limp from the liquor. We started to make out heavily as my lungs felt like they were going to collapse from shortness of breath. She slowly started rubbing me, and as my fingers slipped around her jeans, I started to get hard. Her thong was tight against her ass; I carefully removed it around her legs. I locked the door and reached into my pants; my condom was wrinkled up and I tore it open like a madman. I put it on and spread her legs as she took her shirt off so that I could suck on her nipples. I went deep inside her as she moaned. I thrust back and forth, faster and faster, until I fell back onto the bed. Breathing heavily and sweating from the alcohol, I heard a loud-sounding exhaust coming down the street.

Fuck! It's my dad; I forgot he lives right down the street, I was thinking. I threw my pants and shirt on and ran downstairs to warn everyone.

"My dad's here!" Everyone panicked because they saw me panic. The freshman girls hopped out of the bathroom window, some half-dressed. Everyone else ran out the back door, and I kissed Tiffany before she ran out. The house smelled like pot, there were thongs on the lamps, and my father walked in to see his first-born son hammered and mumbling. I was terrified; maybe it was the fact that Dad was still so young and just had an intimidating look to him. He sat me on the couch as my eyes felt like they were wobbling all over the place.

"You're coming with me," he said.

"No, I'm staying here for Mom," I replied.

"Dude, you're getting in my truck and I'm taking you to my apartment."

I paused and, all of a sudden, felt the words come out of my mouth.

"Fuck that." His eyes lit up as I immediately hopped off the couch and ran out the door with a bottle of liquor in my hand. He chased me down the hill to the school, but I cut through a couple of blocks to Rory's house and got away. I shut off my phone and drank until I passed out at Rory's. *What the hell have I become?* I thought. *Whatever it is that's happening to me, I think I like it.*

CHAPTER 7

THE DARK SIDE

My mother and father knew that I was heading downhill after that night. Mom said that she wanted me to see a psychologist because clearly this divorce was affecting me. To tell you the truth, I was starting to selfishly enjoy my situation; I had an excuse to be bad and to do whatever I wanted.

She took me to a doctor who specialized in kids with divorced parents; Jared was too young, she thought, but I wasn't, especially since I would be turning seventeen soon. The psychologist had me sit down, so I slumped in the chair.

"Logan, why do you feel the need to drink?"

"I don't know; it's fun."

"*Why* is it fun, Logan?"

This lady was irritating me; I pretty much gave her one-word answers as she continued to dig deeper. After a while I grew silent.

After we finished the session, the shrink pulled my mom into her room and had me sit and wait outside. All I could think about was what total bullshit this was to have a stranger judge me, from a couple of silly questions. *How could she possibly know my pain?* She had never walked in my shoes; she just saw a kid on the wrong path and had decided to prescribe him antidepressants.

My mother agreed that I should try them, especially because she had been on them for most of her life. We rode home together, and things felt so different; I couldn't even look my mom in the eyes as she talked to me. She reminded me that her father was very sick, with bipolar disorder and depression. A part of me wanted to hug her and tell her that everything was going to be okay, but I couldn't work up the courage to do so.

The next day, my alarm rang loudly as I woke up and took my first dose of medication from the doctor. I didn't feel anything as I hopped in my van and went to school. I showed up right before the bell rang, so I wouldn't have to see anyone; I just wanted to go to class, and I didn't feel like explaining myself. I totally forgot that my basketball tryouts were that night, though. *Fuck.* After class, I saw the people who were at my party a couple of nights back, and everyone was telling stories about jumping out of the windows and joking about how they wanted to do it again. For once, it felt good to be the guy who threw parties; everyone relied on me to have a good time. I saw my basketball buddies talking in the hallway, and I passed by them quickly—I wasn't sure if they noticed me, but I didn't want to have to explain to them how awful my life had become.

That night, tryouts began, and I was extremely nervous. I hadn't played ball the whole summer and had been partying instead. As we ran up the court, doing drills, my breath was shortened quickly, and my heart was beating out of my chest. We ran a scrimmage: *Ice gets the ball crossover, jump shot and . . . air ball.*

It's okay; it's my just my first shot, I thought, as everyone looked at me, confused. *Ice gets the ball again; crossover . . . shit.* I had lost the ball. I found myself out of breath more easily than usual, and realized that it must have been the cigarettes I had been smoking all summer and continued to smoke, half a pack a day. My lungs were on fire, and my chest felt like it was being ripped apart inside as I ran to the bench with a cramp. There were freshmen who were outplaying me; they seemed hungrier and more ambitious about the game than I was. I was out of shape and no longer the all-star I had been. Tryouts ended and I went home feeling upset, and I think the antidepressant made me even more depressed.

"Life sucks," I said to myself. That night, I felt like I had sunk into a depression hole. Negative thoughts made my eyes water. I was alone in my room and believed that my life was over; I had officially messed it all up. My brother and I never spoke and my father hated me. My mother worked her butt off to support my brother and me, and, in return, I was out getting wasted and letting my brother run around town. My basketball career seemed to be over; I would be very surprised if I had even made the team with the way I had played. I closed my eyes, which filled with tears as I sobbed alone, hoping for a better tomorrow.

Unfortunately, *tomorrow* arrived more quickly than I expected. I woke up and saw that my mom had already left for work. I hopped back in bed and slept all day; I didn't even want to wake up. However, when I finally did, it had to be around three, so I went to Rory's to smoke. We got high for the rest of the night. For three days in a row, I did the same thing. I had missed almost the whole week of school, and didn't want to go anymore. Finally, Thursday arrived and I had to make an appearance. Every one of my teachers pulled me aside and asked me what was going on. I made up a bullshit excuse of how I had the flu. My guidance counselor called me in to chat. I didn't tell him much, but I saw him look in my eyes and judge that I was super depressed.

Later in the day, I heard the announcement that varsity basketball tryouts had been posted. I didn't even want to look, but figured I'd get it over with. I scrolled my finger down the list to see names that were familiar, along with new names, such as the couple of freshmen kids. Then, at the bottom, I saw, *Logan Michaels*.

I was shocked, and didn't know what to expect. I wasn't sure whether I was happy, or frustrated that I had to play for another year. After school, I drove to work to my boring job. I worked with mostly older women in the bakery, so I stayed kind of quiet and kept to myself. I saw Tiffany smile through the glass. I pointed my finger to the back room and she nodded and gestured to meet her in five minutes. We were alone and instantly started to make out and grope each other. I was not sure what was happening or if we were even dating, but I told her that I was having people over to my house again on Friday and that I wanted her to come. She laughed and told me she would be there.

The next day in school, I saw Tim. "Logan, wait up," he said. "Congrats on the team; you excited?"

I laughed and said yes, even though I didn't give a shit. We walked to class like the old days, and he told me about a party that he was having that night. It would be mostly jocks and girls; I figured I could bring Tiffany and show her off.

Tiffany picked me up later that night to go to the party, and I had already gotten alcohol from one of Rory's friends. I had gotten a bottle of Hennessy; it was what I heard in almost every rap song I listened to, so I had to try it. It was expensive for a fifth, though. Tiffany drove us to the party as I took a couple shots. The ride was awesome and I became drunker, smoking cigarettes and taking shots. We pulled up to the party and I rolled in feeling like a million dollars. Tiffany was at my side while everyone who hadn't seen me in a while hugged and high-fived me. *I am the man*, I thought.

I lit a cigarette; my teammates were surprised to see me

smoking, but I didn't care because I was hammered. *Hennessy is fucking awesome,* I said to myself; I had almost finished an entire fifth. My eyes and face grew flushed as Tiffany noticed me starting to stumble. She wanted to get me home by eleven; she said that I was wasted as I stumbled through the house party. We left the party on account of me being wasted and, after hopping in her car, I was hanging out of the window, screaming and shouting. During the ride home, I couldn't keep my hands off of her as I chain-smoked Marlboro Reds. She didn't even want to kiss me because I had smoked so many cigarettes. After she dropped me off, I stumbled up the stairs. My mother was just getting home again as I was coming in the door. I walked past her with my eyes crossed and mumbled gibberish as I fell onto the couch. My mother looked sad; she had just worked a double-shift and got home just in time to see her son puking in a trash bag.

The morning arrived and I was pretty confused about what had happened the night before. *I must have blacked out. Whatever,* I thought, as I went over to Rory's house to take bong rips with him and Tyler. I told them about my night with Hennessy and how awesome it had been. We got another bottle of it that night and invited a bunch of people over to Rory's house. "Round two," I said, as I took a shot of Hennessy and chased it with my medication and a beer. I was falling in love with this lifestyle; I loved getting drunk and high. Nothing mattered as I sipped another beer and smoked a Marlboro Red. There were girls dancing with their shirts off, girls taking shots, and girls making out with each other on the floor. *Who would pass this life up?* I took another shot of Hennessy as I ignored Tiffany's calls; she must have texted me twenty times before I shut my phone off.

I stayed over at Rory's so that my mother wouldn't see me hammered again. The night ended in another blackout; all I remembered was dancing with girls and kissing them, but everything else was a blur. Morning arrived to a slamming headache. I had work in the morning, but I called in sick; first, I was too hung over to work, and second, I didn't feel like explaining myself to Tiffany. Instead, Tyler, Rory, and I just got stoned all day and ate pizza. I was at the point where I smoked weed every day, and ninety percent of my paycheck went to buying weed and alcohol.

The next day at school, my guidance counselor called me in again. He wanted to meet with me on a weekly basis. My grades were going to shit and I was failing a couple of classes. I had over ten absences and tons of tardies. Just to buy myself some time, I blamed it on my parents' divorce. The counselor also mentioned that if my grades continued to slip, I would not be able to play any sports. He was getting on my last nerve, and on top of that, my teachers started to pull me aside after classes to ask if everything was okay. I gave the same excuse of my parents being separated; it was just taking me a little time to adjust. My teachers hated to see me like this.

o o o

On the first day of basketball practice, my coach had us scrimmage. I must have gotten the ball just twice and I couldn't keep up with the team. Luckily, I hit both shots, but was so winded afterward that I could barely play. I began to realize that life continued to move on regardless of whether or not I did; the world didn't revolve around me. The freshman kids were better than me, my old teammates had improved. I didn't even want to be on the team anymore. I jumped into my van after practice, feeling awful. *What's happening to me?*

After a long week of actually attending school, I was completely drained. Practice got worse each day and so did I. The weekend finally arrived and I had patched things up with Tiffany at work—I'd given her some excuse that I slept all night and had been sick. I invited her to another party at my friend Tim's house. It was supposed to be a huge party, and I figured I'd get another bottle of Hennessy, buy two packs of cigarettes, and go to my local pot dealer to get an eighth of weed. It would be a total of eighty dollars spent for recreational purposes.

Tiffany picked up Rory, Tyler, and me. We all started to take shots and drink beers in the car; she didn't really care. We got a nice buzz going before we even got to the party. We finally arrived and saw that there were tons of cars parked everywhere. Tyler and Rory didn't hang out with this crowd too much, but they were always cool when it came to meeting new people. They fit in pretty well. We drank and smoked as the night went on; I would walk around the party with a fifth of Hennessy, sipping it straight out of the bottle. With each sip I took, my emotions and problems vanished.

Now everyone knew me as the guy who drank Hennessy at every party. It had started to become popular as other people began trying my expensive cognac; I passed my bottle around. As the night progressed, I had a serious buzz going, and the party was awesome. Rory, Tyler, and I went outside and smoked a huge joint. I was seriously light-headed as I stumbled back into the party, feeling like an alien. I was so high and drunk that it was as if I was antisocial. All I could do was walk around the party and hear vague sounds as I walked by people; they were talking to me, but I couldn't understand anything as I swallowed my last sip of Hennessy. The last thing I remember was being on the stairs of Tim's house with people surrounding me, and then being brought upstairs and dragging a dresser in front of the door.

Where the hell am I? Why is there a dresser in front of the door and whose room is this? I walked down the stairwell and saw baby pictures of Tim on the wall. *What the hell am I doing here?* I got downstairs and saw that his place was trashed from the party, and there he was, staring at me with a concerned look.

"What's up man?" I said, feeling sick to my stomach.

"Do you remember last night?" he asked.

"Not really," I replied.

"Man, you were messed up," he replied.

"What happened?" I asked.

"You apparently finished your whole fifth of Hennessy by, like, ten o'clock and then smoked outside. You came into the house party and just walked around, not talking to anyone, and then went back outside. No one found you for, like, twenty minutes until Tiffany found you on the stairs in the corner, passed out with two cigs in your hand. She woke you up and you fell on your face as you got up and then you started swearing at her, calling her names."

"Shit."

"Yeah, man, you were bad. You were totally passed out. It was only ten-thirty and everyone was taking selfies with you while you were blacked out. I tried to carry you upstairs to my room so you could sleep, but you fell down the steps. Man, you were so wasted, I couldn't believe it."

"That explains why my whole body is sore," I said and laughed. Tim gave me a ride home later that day, and my mom was home. As she asked me how my night was, I couldn't look at her. I didn't want her to know that her son was a mess and was becoming an alcoholic.

I got my cellphone charged up, and saw that I had a bunch of text messages from Tiffany, Rory, and Tyler, and from some random numbers I didn't even know. Tiffany told me that she didn't want to see me anymore because every time we hung out I was blacked out. It kind of hurt to hear her say that. Rory and Tyler asked how I was feeling and told me to text them. I skipped the next couple days of school and basketball practice, too.

⊙ ⊙ ⊙

On my seventeenth birthday my mother left me a card and kissed me as she went off to work. My brother and father wished me a happy birthday. I tried to ignore my whole family. I wasn't happy with life right now, and knowing I'd have to face another year of all of this brought sadness in my heart. *If I keep going down this path, who knows whether another year would even come?* Then I took the money my mom gave me for my birthday and bought a bag of weed.

After my week-long depression following my birthday, I felt different. I wore a hooded sweatshirt every day to school and never went to classes. I would find ways to skip class and get high outside, along with the burnouts. In the back of my mind, I knew that I needed to stop this or else my life would get worse. But I couldn't stop.

The basketball season had been ongoing for a couple weeks, and I barely played. Coach would only put me in when we had a huge lead. I didn't blame him; my confidence was gone, I could barely make it up and down the court, and my heart wasn't in the game anymore.

I hated the time of the year when the holidays came. I loved my family with all my heart, but couldn't bear for them to see me so changed. I was dreading the holiday when everyone would get together and I would have to go to visit my mom's family first and then my dad's family, and act like everything was okay. They would ask me about basketball, school, girlfriends, and life. I didn't want to explain to them that I had fucked up everything and that it was all going very badly.

When Christmas arrived, my mother begged me to make an appearance, and in my heart I knew that I couldn't let her down. So, what did I do? I went out with Rory, Tyler, and a couple of other pothead buddies to play pool on Christmas night. My heart hurt so much as I smiled and drank the pain away. Each shot I took felt like a dagger, but I just couldn't bear to face my family on Christmas, so I kept drinking.

Christmas season eventually ended and I was relieved. New Year's Eve was a different story, however. Rory had a big party planned for that night; there must have been thirty to forty people there—a mix from burnouts, jocks, freshman, and seniors. As usual, I brought my Hennessy and had some weed ready for the night. Rory's pot dealer came to the party and had brought a couple of his buddies, Sam and Chris. They were a grade older than me and apparently had been heavy into dealing cocaine. I stayed far away from that, though; no way would I put anything up my nose. These guys were both known to fight and brawl with anyone who gave them shit, and they were also known to win every fight.

I became smashed as the night progressed. Walking through the house, I started to hear whispers. It was almost as if everyone around me was blurred out—the room became smaller and I felt as if I was alone.

BOOM! My shoulder bumped into someone at the party and they pushed me down. I felt my face turn beet-red, and adrenaline began pumping through my whole body. I felt like I could pick up a house over my shoulder. I looked up as everyone's faces became clear again, and saw one of the freshman guys on my team staring at me.

"What the fuck," I said, as I ran at him, picked him up in midair, and then body-slammed him onto the table. Everyone looked at me like I was a madman; the girls cleared out and ran outside of the house in a panic. My victim broke away and yelled at me like I was a crazed animal. The scariest thing was that he must have been 6'2" and 250 pounds, but with the Hennessy and all of the hate in my heart, I picked him up like a feather when I smashed him through the table. The poor kid had bumped into me by accident, it turned out, and I had just snapped.

I ran to my van, got in and slammed the door, and burned out of Rory's, hammered. I flew up the street, driving home around midnight. *Great way to start a new year,* I thought as I lit up a cigarette and hit the gas harder. My heart raced; I just wanted to get home and go to bed; I must have been too drunk to function.

I raced past a parked car and looked back to see blue lights flashing. *Fuck!* My heart almost stopped. *I am going to get a DUI and lose my license! Shit.* My foot hit the pedal and I floored it and turned a couple of corners quickly. The cop sped up as I turned another corner, almost flipping my van. The rush was amazing, and I inhaled my cigarette more harshly. I saw an empty driveway across the street, so I flew in there, shut off my lights, and ducked under the steering wheel.

The cop passed slowly, and my heart felt like it was going to explode. I poked my head up briefly and saw his light flashing around. *Shit!* I ducked back and closed my eyes, praying that he had passed. When I looked up again, he was gone. I was only one block away from my house, but I figured I needed to wait it out for a little while. I sat in my van for about thirty minutes, smoking cigarettes. I started the engine, slowly pulled out of the random driveway, and crept around the first street, imagining that the cop would be at every turn. Then the next turn, and the next, until I finally arrived at home and backed up all the way into our dirt driveway, ran inside the house, and passed out.

My body ached and my lungs killed me when I awoke. I must have smoked a pack of cigarettes; I wasn't sure if my run-in with the cop had been a dream. There was only one way to find out—Rory and Tyler. I arrived at Rory's house to find the place still trashed; he hadn't cleaned up at all. There must have been joints everywhere, still lit, and there were beer bottles all over the place. They were just waking up when I walked in, and they laughed when they saw me.

"What happened?" I said, nervously, not sure what I had done. They told me that I did in fact smash someone over the table, breaking it, and then left. About fifteen minutes after I had left and was chased, the same cop had come back to the house party, had arrested and interrogated Rory and Tyler, and had broken up the party. The cop asked what had happened to the table and who drives a maroon van. Rory and Tyler had played dumb. I gasped for a deep breath and high-fived them in relief as we all laughed and lit up a massive blunt.

In my heart, I couldn't believe what I was doing, but I liked the attention my behavior was bringing me. The next week at school, there were people I didn't know talking to me about how hammered I had been and telling me that it was awesome. Most of my jock friends ignored me, and I think I had officially moved to the dark side. I skipped basketball practice that night and skipped school and work for most of the week.

I noticed that my brother was starting to hang out with Vanessa, a girl from his grade. She was the same age as he was, thirteen, and she would come over to the house and do homework with Jared; she was there almost every day. I would say "hi" to her and would then ignore both of them most of the time. I hadn't spoken to Jared in weeks; it hurt so much that we had drifted apart while we were still so young. It seemed like he was spending time with Vanessa to make up for the fact that he had no older brother anymore.

My mother came home one day to find a condom on Jared's bedroom floor. I was shocked when she told me, since he was only thirteen. After all, I had been sixteen and drunk when I first had sex. I knew I should have a talk with him, being the older brother, but, as usual, I left the house and swept my problems under the rug—except under that the rug was usually a blunt.

My father was told about the condom, but he didn't do too much; he would continue to fight with the crazy woman he had been seeing or sleeping with. She continued to threaten to kill my mother, and my father had to get a restraining order against her. Sometimes she would just show up randomly at his house and scream in the street until the cops came and arrested her. She wanted to make his life a living hell, and she succeeded. He had to go to court multiple times for his restraining order, as she always convinced the judge that she was a sweetheart. Maybe because she was sick she knew how to fake it. I didn't see my father too often anymore, so I guess I had no role model either. So finally Jared and I had something in common.

◉ ◉ ◉

The semester was halfway over. I was failing every class except history with Mr. Hillfield, who was hoping I would make it to baseball season. He always looked at me in the hallways, but never questioned me or asked me what was going on. I felt like he was different, as if he actually understood me and knew that talking about my downfall would only make it worse.

Other teachers, of course, looked at me like I was the bad boy in class; at this point, I was sent for detention almost every day, but still didn't go. I would just swear at my teachers and would walk out in the middle of class. The principal couldn't reach me, my parents couldn't reach me—no one could.

During the halfway point of school, the school officer pulled me aside and whispered in my ear, "I know it was you in the van; I will catch you and put you away."

I looked at him, rolled my eyes, and said, "I don't think so."

My heart was dead; I didn't give a fuck about anything anymore. I could either make things right and change my life for the better, or I could go down that dark road. I chose the dark road.

A month later, my mother's worst fear had come true—I was gone and couldn't return and didn't want to. I had thrown everything away and, when I caught her crying one night I just left for Rory's house. I had officially dropped out of school, had quit the basketball and baseball team, and quit my job at Butcher Boy. I had dropped out simply by not showing up to school or basketball anymore. I had never said a word to my coach or teachers.

The antidepressant wasn't helping me, so I stopped taking it and refused to see a counselor again. While my mother worked double shifts, I would have everyone over to the house. Rory, Tyler, and a couple of other friends dropped out with me. We were all bad for each other; we would get high all day, starting in the morning, and then drink when we could afford alcohol. I was unemployed and had to figure out some way to support my habits. Rory and I would drive around in my van, smoking pot while I filled out job applications. I ended up finding a convenience store in the next town over where I would work part-time just to afford weed, alcohol, and gas. It was a job for a loser, but I guess that loser was me. The manager was a dropout, too; he had to be about twenty-five and had red hair and freckles. We hit it off immediately, and he hired me on the spot.

I worked three days a week and on my off-time I was getting high and drunk with the dropout crew. We had a lot of idle time, so we started to get into more trouble than usual. I mean, we were seventeen- and eighteen-year-old kids. My brother continued to see his girlfriend every day. I just hoped that he wouldn't get her pregnant.

My brother was exposed to my party environment, which I always regretted. He would sit upstairs in his room while I had parties with kids stripping, drinking, and smoking, and with people hanging out in the street outside of the house, the madhouse. I made him stay upstairs; sometimes I'd see him downstairs and would yell at him to go back up. He was on probation until he was eighteen, and I didn't want him getting in trouble again. The smart thing for me to do would be to stop having parties, especially when my poor mother was working all night.

The neighbors thought my mother was terrible because of these parties, but she couldn't control me; she worked so much to support us that what happened while she was at work was out of her control. She would come home and sleep and then return to work, but at least she really loved what she did. She was the most popular nurse anywhere she went; it was because her heart was filled with so much love. I knew that whatever road I took, she would support me. I was still her baby boy.

Summer was approaching, which meant trouble was coming. School had finished up, but of course I didn't give a shit; I hadn't been to school for months. The dropout crew was about five people deep and we all had a big summer ready for ourselves: house parties at my place, ragers at Rory's place, and high school parties even though we had dropped out. Surprisingly, my van was still running, even though it was a piece of shit. I took the back seats out and put two beanbags in their place.

The summer of seventeen. My world had collapsed, but a new road had opened up. Rory and I met two girls, Kate and Molly, who always wanted to hang out, get drunk, have sex, and get high. One of the first nights I can remember from that summer involved the four of us. My mother and Rory's were home, for once. So we loaded up my car with alcohol and weed, and the girls jumped onto the beanbags as we opened up the cheap vodka. My heart was racing, and I was hoping I would get drunk and get laid—the perfect night for an adolescent. We had heard about these abandoned apartments one town over, so we decided to drive over there and check it out. When we got there, we crept up slowly in my maroon van as we all laughed nervously.

"The coast is clear," Rory said. We went inside and there wasn't a peep; there were just a couple of couches that were surprisingly clean. We brought in the alcohol and weed, celebrating. Rory rolled up a huge joint as I poured shots for the girls. We must have drunk half the bottle. We were just four young, horny kids messing around. Rory and I argued over who would try to hook up with which girl. I didn't really care.

"Fuck it," I said as Molly came over to me on the couch. She looked so good tonight; maybe it was the alcohol, but she had big, wet lips that I wanted around my dick. "Take them off," I mumbled drunkenly and laughed. She laughed too, then slid my pants off and started to suck and stroke me. I was sure that Rory was in the other room doing the same. Thankfully, I lasted a while because of the liquor in my system. She licked her lips as I pulled up my pants.

"Shit!" Molly gasped, looking at her phone, "It's two; I need to get home!" We jumped in the van and tucked the open bottle of vodka under the seat. I mean, there was still some left and I wanted it.

"Holy shit, I'm hammered," I said and laughed as I looked back at the girls and Rory. After I dropped off Rory, my vision blurred but I nervously started to drive the girls home. *Almost there*, I thought as my vision was going. I was legitimately afraid that I was going to pass out and fail to get these girls home safely.

BOOM! SCRATCH! Fuck. I did pass out for a whole minute, and I woke up to see that I was scraping a bunch of parked cars along the road. *Holy shit, what am I doing?* I pulled up to the girls' houses at two-thirty, and luckily got them home after scraping ten cars on the side of the street.

Two more blocks to go, and I'm home free; thank God. As I drove slowly with both hands on the wheel, I noticed a car behind me. My eyes sobered up at once, my chest stuck out straight, and I felt like I had swallowed my tongue. The cops were trailing me! I continued to drive cautiously as the police car pulled up closer and flashed his blue lights. *OMG; my life's over,* I thought, *I have a bottle of booze under my seat and weed in the car, not to mention that I'm hammered.*

"Driver, get home immediately," I heard out of his telecom.

You have to be kidding me, I mumbled under my breath. The ride home was just five minutes, but felt like it would never end.

Have you ever been so drunk that you thought the night before had been a dream? Yeah, it had been one of those nights. The next morning I ran outside to my van to see if I had dreamed that I smashed into ten cars last night. *PHEW! Wait, shit, my rearview mirror fell off; wow, it had happened.* "Screw it," I said, and drove over to Rory's to tell him the story and to get high. You would have thought after that I might have toned it down a little, but I didn't.

Since we had found our great abandoned hideout, we decided to throw parties there every night. Kids from town would join us and we would drink, smoke, and hook up; it was a blast to have fun without cops breaking up our parties. However, on a night about midway through the summer, we must have been followed.

It must have been around ten p.m., and we were partying and having a good time until we heard sirens. Seemingly out of nowhere, the cops busted in the door. I immediately put my car keys in my sock; I didn't want the police to know I would be driving. Of course, it was the school officer who had said he would be watching me.

"Logan Michaels, I knew you would mess up eventually," he said snidely. I rolled my eyes and acted like I wasn't fazed; after all, I hadn't been caught yet.

"Show me your keys," he said.

"I didn't drive here," I replied.

"Bullshit," he said. He then patted me down in front of the whole party and found nothing. He told everyone else to get out of there if they didn't want to be arrested. Little did he know that right after he left, I jumped into my van and took off, laughing. Rory lit up a blunt with a couple of girls and drove in the other direction. *The cops can't stop me; the adventure makes me feel alive. Who needs school? I want the life of an outlaw....*

CHAPTER 8

BAD BOYS DON'T GO TO HEAVEN

If there was an award for worst role model, I definitely would have won it. My brother and I didn't talk much anymore. I would walk by him and ignore him; he would spend all of his time with his girlfriend. My father tried to spend time with Jared and me as often as he could. Jared was still angry with Dad and wanted nothing to do with him. I didn't really talk to my father anymore; I was angry at him, too, but honestly it didn't bother me that much. I loved having the freedom and parties, and I figured I'd let him live his life and I'd live mine. My life, of course, could have used a lot of guidance and direction from a role model, which I didn't have. But at my age, even if I had, would I really have listened?

It was the end of my summer of being seventeen, probably a couple of weeks after I crashed my van against all of those cars. It was Rory, Tyler, and me all hanging at Rory's house.

Rory said that his pot dealer had just gotten some mushrooms, and of course I'd heard about them, but had never actually tried them. We got a little over an eighth of them; they looked like actual mushrooms, except they were dirty and smelled awful. I had heard that they would make you hallucinate and trip pretty hard. I was nervous to take them at first, but was so depressed from life in general that I figured, *how could it get any worse?*

We each ate a handful of the mushrooms. They tasted dry and gross, and were mushy and crunchy as they went down my throat. I had to swallow them with a huge glass of water. We all waited aimlessly on the couch, watching TV; I must have asked Rory and Tyler a thousand time how long it would take to kick in. Yeah, I was *that* guy. The air was crisp and the screen door at Rory's creaked louder and louder.

We were watching *Master Chef* as the drugs started to kick in. I found myself amazed, watching a simple dish being cooked. My jaw felt like it had dropped down to the floor and I couldn't stop laughing with excitement. The walls started to show images and I thought I was losing my mind. *This isn't reality; what is life? What's the whole point to this?* Everything felt so lucid and like a wonderland as we all realized we were each "tripping balls," as the kids would say. After tripping for about an hour, we decided to go outside, and I remember walking down the street feeling like I was the only man on earth, or like I was an alien from outer space. We walked a mile to the woods, where there was a huge hill. We hiked up the whole hill like three men on a mission, having no clue why we were doing it. Finally, we arrived at the top; we had reached our destination. As I looked up at the stars, I could swear God was talking to me; He said something, but I couldn't hear, and then I looked over at Tyler and Rory as they started to roll down the hill. I laughed and joined them; we rolled all the way to the bottom, cracking up.

"Mushrooms are the shit," we all laughed as we hit the

bottom of the hill. This, of course, was the first of the many times that I did mushrooms.

By the end of the summer, my mother knew that I was drinking and smoking, and she had a feeling that I was starting to explore other drugs. She tried her hardest to stop me, and told me that I needed to live with my family. That conversation still haunts me, as I can remember the scene so vividly. I arrived home one night, high out of my mind; I mean, my eyes looked like they were bleeding red.

"Why are your eyes so red, Logan? Why are you doing this to yourself?"

"Leave me alone, mom!"

"You need to live with your father for discipline. I can't stop you anymore."

"Fuck that. I'm not living with him."

"If you don't, I'm kicking you out."

"Sounds great," I replied, as I slammed the front door shut and drove to Rory's house.

I can't imagine how long my mother cried after she watched her first son leaving. Rory accepted me, of course, and said that I could crash on his couch. I didn't move completely into his house, but I never visited my mother; I would only stop by the house to get food while she was working. I left Jared alone as his relationship with Vanessa grew stronger; they were almost inseparable. He continued to do community service three days a week. My father tried calling me because my mother had told him what had happened, but I ignored his calls; I didn't feel like getting lectured.

Rory, Tyler, and I took a little trip one night. We were smoking at Rory's house and taking shots, but we found ourselves bored. We decided to hop in my van and take a cruise. We had a bottle of vodka that we put in a bucket of ice under my seat. We rolled a blunt and lit up as I drove aimlessly.

"Where the fuck are we?" Tyler asked. We all laughed as I saw a sign for a town; I had no clue where I was. Eventually, we found our way back to the neighboring town, North Reading.

"Fuck, Rory, put the bottle away. Hide the weed," I said, cursing again and throwing on my seatbelt. Blue lights were approaching us from behind and I pulled over, thinking this would be the time that I would lose my license. We had vodka on ice under my seat, weed in my glove compartment, and we were all, of course, drunk and high.

"How are you, officer?" I asked.

"Step out of the car, all of you." There we were, the all-star team, sobered up instantly with two cops interrogating us. "Do you know why I stopped you?" asked the first.

"Not sure, officer," I replied.

"Well, a couple reasons; It's three in the morning and you're driving and, second, you had no lights on while driving."

I'm such a fucking idiot, I thought, but quickly replied, "We all just got in a fight with our girlfriends, so we just wanted to take a drive to clear our heads. And also I've been having issues with the lights; I need to get them fixed." There was a silence afterward, as I could feel my heart racing to the point where I thought I was going to have a heart attack, and my knees felt like they were going to collapse from the anxiety.

The officer replied, "Well, leave your car in the parking lot. We are going to take you to the station and have your parents pick you up."

I left my van in the parking lot as the police took us to the station in their squad car. I guess I couldn't complain because they never searched my car, but I still had a bottle of vodka sitting in there under the seat, and weed in the glove compartment; I needed to get that out of there before they found it.

We arrived at the station; it was the first time I had ever been there and we were so high and drunk that I don't know why the cops didn't arrest us. They stood right behind Rory as he called his parents; his mom picked up, yelling at him, but said that she'd take him home anyway. Tyler's parents were out and he needed to get a ride from Rory's mom. I was next; I dialed the phone as I could feel the heat of the cop behind me. I thought my mother was going to kill me; I had left her house and now was calling from a police station—she didn't need this shit. First ring, she picked up, and I hung it up quickly, prompting the officer to ask what had happened.

"Call again," he said, as I swallowed my tongue and dialed a fake number.

"No answer, officer," I said.

"Dial one more time and put it on speaker phone," he said. I could feel my face flush and my heart sped up like I had just run an hour-long marathon.

Here goes nothing, I thought as I dialed my mom's number for real. *No answer, thank God.* I got a ride home with Rory's mom and crashed on their couch that night, but all I could think about was how I would get my van.

First thing the next morning I said, "Rory, wake up! We need to take your mom's car to get my van."

We slowly started his mom's car at six a.m., knowing that she wouldn't wake up until around eight. We drove to the parking lot where my car was, thankfully, still parked. I jumped in it right away and took off, driving to Rory's house. We had made it back just before his mother woke up. I was hoping the cops wouldn't realize the next day that my van was moved. The cops, however, never called or showed up; I couldn't believe that I had gotten away again. I should probably have lost my license by now, but my mother never found out. Of course, what goes around comes around. I was not sure if I had believed in karma before, but a week later, I would start to believe in it.

⊙ ⊙ ⊙

Summer was coming to an end soon, but, honestly, it didn't even matter because I wasn't returning to school and I was working as a cashier at the convenience store. I could get high and ring people's items up all the time. Plus, the store I worked for sold beer, so I would grab a six-pack and a pack of cigarettes every night and just leave the money in the drawer. Of course, there were cameras, but I had been doing this throughout the summer and had yet to be caught. I would also scratch tickets and "forget" to count them when I totaled up the day's lottery sales. I was a degenerate when it came to scratching those tickets.

My buddies would come into the store some nights when I was working. Of course, we were only seventeen, but I would sell them alcohol anyway. I'm surprised that the store didn't get shut down; there must have been kids who looked like babies walking out with thirty-packs of beer. I even sold beer to my younger cousin who was sixteen and lived in the town. Her girlfriends would come in and buy alcohol, their friends would come in; I would sell to anyone—what did I care?

Like they say, bad things come in threes, and they sure did for me. I arrived at work for my shift, and my manager was there. He looked at me, concerned and nervous.

"What's up?" I said.

He replied seriously, "We need to talk."

I played it off cool, knowing that he had probably found out everything.

"You know the cameras haven't been working, so I don't know what else you have been doing, but I totaled up the quarter in lottery sales and we were short over one thousand dollars, unaccounted for. The beer and cigarettes have been off track, too. Listen, I'm not sure what you're doing, and I think you're a good kid, but I have to let you go."

I thought, *thank God, I probably could have been arrested or sued.* I shook his hand and casually hopped back in my van. *It had been a shitty job anyway,* I thought as I pulled out. The only problem was that I needed money for my usual alcohol, weed, and gas, plus money for munchies. *I'll figure something out later.*

I went over to Rory's to smoke a blunt. I decided that I wanted to drive around our town and get high, fish-bowling my van. After smoking most of the blunt, we realized that we were in the middle of downtown North Andover, with my car completely filled with smoke from weed. Blue lights flashed, and I was pulled over with a blunt still burning in the ashtray. *How the hell am I going to get away with this one?* I wondered.

The officer approached casually, and as I rolled my window down, smoke poured into his face. *No fucking way*; it was the officer from school who hated me.

"Finally," he said as he took me out of the car and searched me from head to toe right on the side of the street. I was so embarrassed; I looked like a bum, wearing sweatpants and a hooded sweatshirt with the hood pulled over my head. It was like I was on an episode of *Cops.*

He then proceeded to rip my car apart, more than he needed to. He found the blunt burning in the ashtray and smiled. He loved to see me struggling. He took me into his police car, but not the back seat—the front seat.

He turned toward me and said: "Listen, maybe we can make a deal."

I looked him in the eyes as he stared back into my bloodshot ones; I couldn't believe this was happening. I was so high, and I was sitting in the front seat with a cop.

"If you tell me who is supplying the marijuana to the high school, I will let you go and won't even send you to court," he said. Maybe this would have worked on a wimp, but I replied differently.

"No clue, officer; I can't help you."

He replied, "Okay, then I will see you in court for possession." He took my weed and followed me home; of course, I was kicked out of Rory's, so I had to go to my mom's house. Not only did this cop know where I lived now, but he had also forced me to go inside and see my mother.

My mom was fortunately the most forgiving person. She hugged me and told me that she loved me. I loved her so much deep down inside, and it was just that I was depressed with my own life at this time. I couldn't give her any love because I had no love in my heart—only anger and hate.

I was arraigned and had a hearing in two weeks, and I was dreading it. I drove with Rory to the Lawrence District Court. It was filled with criminals and punks like me, but for some reason I knew that I was more than what I had become. *I don't belong here*, I thought as I saw kids with gang tattoos, and other people who looked really rough.

"Logan Michaels," my name was called. My heart was racing as I stood up with my lawyer. He was a family lawyer; he knew my mother's brother pretty well and was doing us a favor by defending me. He told me to just plead guilty, promising that he would take care of the rest.

"How do you plead, Mr. Michaels?"

"Guilty, your honor."

My lawyer then made his statement: "Your honor, my client is recently undergoing his parents' divorce, and this is his first time being arrested." The judge gave me a break and fined me two hundred dollars. *That was it?* I had gotten off easy compared to other kids; maybe the judge could tell that I was a good kid? I shook my lawyer's hand and left the court. I never wanted to go back to that place; it was very depressing and gave me anxiety.

The second time that I did mushrooms must have been two weeks after my court hearing. I was feeling kind of sad because school had started and I didn't go anymore. One night, Rory, Tyler, and I met up with a couple of buddies who had also dropped out, and we all went to a high school hockey game. We started to pregame at another kid's house whose parents were gone. He had almost a pound of mushrooms that he was trying to sell. We bought a bag off him and took the drugs right before we drove to the game. Driving on mushrooms was one of the funniest experiences. I didn't care what happened to me anymore. We had all jumped in my van and I started to drive; I felt like I was in a video game while driving down the street. We arrived at the game as we were tripping our asses off, walking into the crowd of people I hadn't seen all summer.

I felt so alien when I walked in, like everyone was staring at me. The game was starting and everyone stood up for the Pledge of Allegiance. We all sat there in the corner with our hoodies pulled over our heads. Everyone must have known we were on something; we were the only five guys sitting in the whole crowd.

Halfway through the game, Rory tapped me on the shoulder and said, "Follow me." He walked quietly into the hallway and then into the other team's locker room. It was quiet and no one was in there. He rifled through the other team's wallets and bags, stealing about one hundred bucks. It was a crazy rush as we ran outside, called the guys, and took off. We laughed as we drove off with the stolen money.

In celebration of that, we called up a couple of girls who were always up for sex and, for old time's sake, we had a party at the abandoned house we used to go to. What did we do with the money? I'll break it down:

$35 for a bag of mushrooms
$30 for a handle of vodka and chasers
$20 for a gram of marijuana
$15 for snacks

Knowing that it wasn't our money made everything so much

better. We rolled a blunt and took more mushrooms before the girls arrived. We took shots until we were fucked up. The night was amazing; we were tripping, high, and drunk, having a blast. We all got laid that night, too. Sex on mushrooms was unreal; it almost felt as though it wasn't even happening, and the adrenaline was almost too much. The girls went home that night and we ended up passing out there on the floor. The morning arrived, pouring with rain and an awful hangover to go with it. It was dreadful out, and the after-affect from mushrooms was miserable; it would bring us back to reality.

The reality was that I couldn't picture myself ever getting out of this hole that I was in. I was heading for rock bottom and couldn't stop myself; I was so depressed that I didn't even want to wake up anymore.

Of course, the situation immediately got worse. Rory and I pulled out in the rain and, as I came around the corner in my van doing sixty miles per hour—I don't know what set me off—I just hit the gas and we swerved into a huge dirt hill; my van jumped into the air. I tried to back out, but the van was stuck halfway in midair.

"Fuck," I said as I tried to back up for 30 minutes straight. Rory and I sat in the car, not knowing what to do, and then the worst thing I could imagine happened. I noticed a beige Chevy truck drive by slowly; I looked into the driver's side window and saw my biggest nightmare.

My father slammed on his brakes and hopped out of the car to ask what happened. Rory and I were still kind of buzzing from the night before. I told him that I had just lost control and he looked at me, knowing right away that I was bullshitting him. He then tied a rope to the van and towed us out; I guess it was better him than the cops.

Surprisingly, he wasn't that mad; he followed me home and told me that he needed to talk with me that night, that it was very important and he would pick me up around six. I couldn't avoid it, since he had decided to help me out. I figured that it would be a huge lecture about how I was pretty much throwing my life away.

Jared arrived home from school that day and told me that Dad wanted to speak with both of us. Now I was more concerned, and figured it could be about the girl who was stalking my mother. I hadn't heard too much about her lately because I had tried to ignore that it was even happening.

Six o'clock struck as Jared and I waited on the couch for my father. He arrived about fifteen minutes later. We went to his house for the usual dinner, which was either hot dogs and beans, or spaghetti. After the awkward dinner phase, we all sat on the couch and he told us the news that changed our lives forever.

He said, "Of course, you know about the woman who I had been seeing." We both shook our heads, trying to ignore him. "Well, I wanted to tell you sooner, but didn't know how. I just told your mother and told her to wait until I told you guys."

My chest tightened as my knees shook nervously. *What the hell could it be?* My father looked more nervous than me and Jared.

"You have a half sister."

The look in Jared's eyes was indescribable; he looked as if he wanted to cry and scream at my dad at the same time, but he managed to say nothing. My stomach felt sick and I was speechless.

"What's her name?" I finally mumbled like a little kid.

"Her name is Emma," he replied. I didn't know how to take this in; how was I supposed to feel? I mean, a sister by another woman?

My brother showed no emotion that night when we both arrived home and saw our mom. I stayed in bed staring at the wall, thinking about how I had always wanted a sister. *But why did it have to happen this way?* I couldn't imagine the pain my mother was feeling inside. It turned out, I had had a sister for close to a year now and I hadn't even met her; I was not sure if

I even wanted to see her, but I hoped that when she got older we could be friends. Not to mention that, because of this, my mother had put the house up for sale and now had to look for an apartment for us. We all put our problems aside that night.

A month later, the house had been sold and my mother had found a three-bedroom in North Andover for the three of us. It was pretty expensive, but she had a career now and could make ends meet. It was right near the high school, which kind of made me sick because I could see all of the kids I used to play sports with as they drove past our place to go to school. I felt as though they were moving on while I was going backwards in time—*that should have been me.*

The night we moved in, my mother and I had a long talk about my brother and me. Mom told me news about Jared that I didn't want to hear, especially since I had been a shitty role model.

"I found a marijuana pipe in Jared's room the other day."

I closed my eyes slowly and took a deep breath, knowing he was on the wrong track now. The mature thing to do would be to talk to Jared about this, but instead I swept it under the rug like usual. My mom also talked about me getting back on my feet and working; she said that if I was not going to school then I need to work and support myself. The part of the conversation that surprised me was that she and Dad had talked, and together they had bought me a ticket to Germany. *Germany?*

Probably about six months back, my buddy Greg had stayed with a transfer student in Bonn, and he had had a blast over there. He said that he was going back and that he wanted me to stay with him and the transfer student in Germany. My parents said that they would think about it. However, since I had dropped out, I wasn't expecting that they would let me go. I think that my parents had thought it would be good for me if I got away for a while. The two-week trip would happen in three months. I felt so awful knowing that I had put my mom through hell, and she was sending me on my dream vacation anyway. I hoped that one day I could make it up to her and make her proud of her son.

Of course, the first thing I needed to do was to get another job. Where was a high school dropout to begin? I didn't have too many options. Rory told me about a moving company a couple towns over that paid well and was easy; it basically just involved moving furniture all day. The problem here was that I no longer had a car, so I had to borrow my mother's car to interview for the position and fill out an application.

My mother let me drive her new black Camry. Surprisingly, there was no interview; it was just me filling out an application and a couple of personal questions. I figured that I had done my due diligence and would wait to hear back from them in a couple days, like they had said.

After I had filled out my application, I figured that I could kill some time and go over to Rory's house. Tyler and he were there like usual, watching TV and smoking pot. I took a couple of hits and talked about the day.

"Hey, let's take a cruise," Tyler said.

"Nah, I have my mom's car," I replied. But eventually, Tyler persuaded me to go with him by promising to roll a joint, since I really didn't have much money left. We all jumped in my mom's car and lit up the joint; I figured we could just air out the car later. After we got stoned, Tyler thought of a crazy idea. He claimed he had done it a bunch of times before and had never been caught.

"Let's got to Bob's," he said, talking about the nearby clothing store, "And steal some new shoes. I heard there are these new Nikes that are unreal."

I looked down at my old pair of Nikes that were beat-up, covered in grass stains and falling apart. "Let's try it," I said.

Rory disagreed for once and sat in the car while Tyler and I went in. We both walked in, stoned, with our hands in our pockets. I followed Tyler to the shoe department as he sat down after finding the new Nikes that were spotless and pure white. After finding his size, he tried them on and slipped his old pair into the box.

"That's it? Are you sure this works?" I said.

"Yeah, I've done it a bunch of times." Eleven and a half; perfect, they had my size, one more pair. I slipped off my old, dirty shoes and put on the crisp and comfortable white Nikes. They felt amazing as I stood up. With each step we took toward the store's exit, I could feel my heart pounding, but on the surface I looked calm. Finally we were close to the front door; only ten more feet to go. *Oh my God, we did it!*

"Hold it right there, boys!" *No fuckin' way!* Two men were at the entry of the building as we slowly walked by them. *Busted!* They took us into the back security room and played the video of Tyler and me putting our old shoes into the shoeboxes. Tyler panicked and begged the cop not to arrest him, as he was already on probation multiple times for possession of marijuana. I sat, slumped, as they handcuffed me, and closed my eyes in despair. *What am I doing?*

I was embarrassed as the two officers arrived to walk Tyler and me out in handcuffs. I could hear the mutters from onlookers, no doubt judging us as losers. If only the cops and crowd knew that, only a year ago, I had been an all-star and that I used to earn great grades and had a great life. *People only judge a book by its cover,* I reminded myself as I slumped my head down and got shoved in the cop car.

◎ ◎ ◎

Technically, I was arrested in New Hampshire, which was one state over from Massachusetts. It was only twenty minutes from my town, though. Apparently, in New Hampshire, they try you as an adult when you are seventeen, unlike in Massachusetts, where you're considered an adult in the eyes of the law only when you reach eighteen. After they took fingerprints, took our pictures, and put Tyler and me in a cell, they called my mother.

My mother arrived at the station in her nursing uniform; she had been ready to go to work, but had needed to call out, due to the fact that her son had been arrested. They told her that if she didn't pay five hundred dollars in bail money for me, that I would be going to Essex County Jail. Essex County is a pretty tough jail for criminals who commit crimes ranging from burglary to murder and rape, and to think that I would be going there for stealing shoes blew my mind. I was scared that I would be in jail alongside guys much harder than myself. My father had told my mother to let them send me there, saying that I needed to learn a lesson.

I agree that I did need to learn a lesson, and maybe this would have changed my perspective on things. However, I knew kids who had gone into jail and came out worse; jail only surrounds you with more criminals. But my mother paid the bail and took me home that day with a warning. I sat in her car with my head down during the whole ride; I had nothing to say; an apology was useless. I could tell that my mother wanted to break down in tears. At times, I wondered which was more difficult: me struggling and losing everything or her having to watch it happen gradually over these rough years. My heart was dead. I was in denial, and so low that it hurt every night to think of my reality. Getting high, as always, took the pain away.

I sat upstairs in my room for the next couple of days. I watched the cars pass as they drove to the high school. Winter was coming, and I had no car, no job, and not a penny to my name. My brother stayed in his bedroom with Vanessa; my mother and I could hear them having sex some nights, and could sometimes smell marijuana. He continued to go to school and amazingly got good grades—he was always a smart kid. I think it was good that at least he had Vanessa, because if he didn't have her shoulder to lean on, he probably would have been like me.

I was single; every girl that I hooked up with or entered a relationship with eventually left me because I was always drunk or high. I cared more about getting trashed than about being in a relationship. Of course, I had hookups here and there, mainly because I partied a lot, but I hadn't experienced true love, and I wouldn't admit that I wanted it.

I was back on the scene before long, and on my first night back I went hard. Tyler called me on a Friday night; my mother was working and my brother was home with Vanessa. He asked me if I wanted to get drunk and said that he had a surprise for me. He showed up about an hour later with a bottle of Grey Goose vodka and a twelve-pack of Bud Light.

We took a couple shots in my room to loosen up. Tyler had a gram of white powder that smelled like gasoline when you got close to it. So far, I had only seen cocaine in movies, but never would have thought to put it up my nose. But then Tyler poured some of it into a pile on a table, took out his debit card, and started crushing it up. He divided two lines equally.

"No, man, let me just try a small one first," I said. He laughed as he snorted a line and his eyes watered up. He smiled, but he had a serious look.

"Woo," he said as he snorted. "What a drip."

I rolled up a dollar bill tightly after watching Tyler do it. I nervously stuck the bill into my nose and proceeded to the line.

"Here goes . . ." *SNIFF!* Adrenaline rushed to my heart as my blood pumped with excitement; *holy shit!*

"I can taste it in the back of my throat," I said to Tyler.

"Good, right? That's the drip. Here, put some on your teeth; it will numb your mouth."

"My throat is numb, is that normal?" I asked.

"Yeah, that means it's good," Tyler replied. We smoked a couple cigarettes back to back; it was incredible. Our eyes swelled up to double their size and we were officially, as they would say, "yayed out."

Tyler and I shared heartfelt stories like we were the only two guys on earth; I learned coke does that to you. We continued to get fucked up as we smoked a blunt and took shots of Grey Goose. About an hour later, I found myself hurting for another line and so did Tyler. We blew another one, except it was a little bigger this time. The rush was amazing and woke me right back up as I drank. *I feel like I could drink forever on this stuff.*

Tyler and I did our last line of the gram as three-thirty in the morning arrived, and we were binged out. I tried to fall asleep that night, but all I could feel was my heart pounding and racing, which was keeping my eyes open. I didn't get much sleep, but it had been an amazing experience.

Rory wasn't about cocaine; for some reason, he never wanted to put anything up his nose, so he stuck mostly to weed. Tyler and I did it a couple weekends back and forth, but after that it became a little too expensive, so we cut back. The last night we did it, however, was right before my eighteenth birthday. Tyler came over to my house while my mom was working. We started drinking and smoking and then decided we needed some cocaine. He called some local guy who had dropped out a while back; he must have been twenty-two and now sold cocaine.

Tyler told me he could get us a gram, but that we needed to be there in fifteen minutes. My mother had just come home from work and had gone to bed. The drop was about a mile away, and if we walked, we probably wouldn't make it. "Fuck, what we are going to do?"

"I need to do a line, Tyler." Then I saw an idea pop into my head. My mother's keys were in her pocketbook, just sitting there. The only problem here was that my mother's bedroom window was right next to the driveway, and she might hear her car starting.

"Here's the plan, Tyler," I began. "I am going to put the keys in and put the car in neutral. Then I want you to push it back into the road, and we can start it there."

The idea worked brilliantly; as I started the car in the street, I was hammered and high.

"I can't believe I'm doing this, but I need that drip."

Tyler and I drove to the building where his dealer was; he told us to come in and get it. I still get haunted by the apartment building he lived in—I had felt like a junkie. We parked the car in the lot next to an abandoned dumpster. We walked up stairs that were old and had splinters coming out of them; the hallway had paint chips falling off of its walls and the building smelled like lost dreams.

There he was, the cocaine dealer. He had dirty-blond hair and his apartment was disgusting, with pizza boxes and plates everywhere. It stank of stale food and marijuana.

"You just made it," he said, "But I only have half a gram, I did the other." His eyes looked like two golf balls, bloodshot, and he had a creepy look to him. We were both too scared to argue with him because he could probably kill us. He crunched up the last of his cocaine, which amounted to three massive lines. He said that we could do it there if we wanted. *Fuck it, where else was I going to do it?*

Tyler blew the first one and his eyes opened up wide; he looked like he just sprung out of bed. *Wow!* He lit up a cigarette immediately after, and took a shot of Jägermeister that the dealer provided us. *SNIFF!* "Chase it with Jägermeister," he said. My eyes opened just as wide as Tyler's while my heart raced with adrenaline. *It's all worth it,* I thought.

After we chilled for about a half hour we needed to leave. We hopped in my mom's car and both went for our packs of cigarettes. *Fuck!* We both had none.

"I need one, Tyler," I said.

"Me too, but there's a convenience store open 24/7 ten minutes away." Being that it was two in the morning it was our only option, and we were both so yayed up that we needed a cigarette. I knew that if I got pulled over, my life would be over and my mother would kill me, but cocaine is a strong drug and I didn't think that far ahead. We made it to the store, and I lit up a wonderful Marlboro Red. The rain started to come down pretty hard and I just wanted to get home and return my mom's car before she found out.

I decided to take the highway because my street was right off the exit so it would be a lot quicker. We jumped onto I-95 North and I hit the gas as we approached the ramp. We got closer to the ramp as I hit the gas harder and harder—it must have been the cocaine. I reached about sixty while merging onto the highway as the turn got thinner and the rain hit the tires. We hit the ramp, spinning us into the middle of the highway, which dipped us down into the grass about five feet from the road. We both held our breath as the car stopped; my heart felt like it was going to explode. I saw my life flash by in an instant: my brother and me playing Frisbee down on the Cape, all of the good times, and then my mother crying. . . .

Tyler and I were silent during the ride home. We were lucky there had been no oncoming traffic, otherwise we would have been dead. The car was a little bit scratched up when I returned it to the driveway, and one wheel was shaking pretty badly.

Tyler walked home, and I went in the house and went to bed, hoping that I would wake up to find that none of this had really happened. The morning came and my mother went out to her car, and immediately came back inside. I walked outside to look at the damage I had done, and saw the scrapes on the side of the door, the smashed fender, the damaged wheel, and the huge cigarette burn hole in the back seat. I couldn't even look my mother in the eye; I wanted to die. She was speechless and almost broke into tears. She then told me she was thankful that I didn't kill myself. I promised that I would pay for it, but she knew that I wouldn't be able to; she walked back inside the house.

I went over to Rory's and Tyler's house to get high and to forget what just happened. I got drunk later that night to the point where I barely could walk home. I stumbled through the baseball field and fell down a couple of times and could swear I blacked out. I sat on the bleachers by myself, with my head down and my hooded sweatshirt on, looking at the baseball field. I was at rock bottom, and didn't know what to do anymore; I couldn't imagine my life continuing like this—I would be dead. Eventually, I made it home somehow and woke up the next day, on my eighteenth birthday, to a letter on the toilet and a happy birthday card.

CHAPTER 9

THE WORLD STOLE MY SPIRIT

My mother was at work, but she had left me a note that brought tears to my eyes:

Logan,

Happy Eighteenth Birthday! I know things have been hard on you these past couple years. I remember holding you in my arms like you were a baby just yesterday. I love you with all my heart and it breaks my heart to see you drunk and high all the time. You are a wonderful young man with so much potential. I remember you being a perfectionist and organizing your baseball cards and playing basketball in the yard for hours. You always excelled at anything you did and never let the world bring you down no matter what. I cry thinking of what you're going through some nights, I cry knowing that you lost your father and knowing that so many bad things have happened over these years. Most sadly, I cry because you're a handsome young man who deserves a beautiful woman in his life, but you drink just to feel at peace. Please, Logan, I hope one day you realize I will be here for you no matter what you become in this life, but I just want you to become happy. You have some much potential Logan Michaels, please use it. I love you so much and forever. Happy Birthday.

Love,
Mom

I must have cried in my bed for an hour straight after reading that note. I finally realized that my mother understood what I was going through. Before my mother was a nurse, she used to work part-time at group homes for kids who had even worse situations than I did now. She could relate to any young person and make them feel at ease, and she could always put my heart at rest. She was the most understanding woman in the world. She had once told me that someday, if she didn't become a nurse, then she wanted to become a psychiatrist.

I saw Mom when she got home from work, and hugged her so tightly and apologized for everything. She knew how much I loved her; I just wish I could show it more. My father came by and wished me a happy birthday. It was good to see the family together again like old times; I missed that. My father and mother said that they were going to put their money together and help me buy a car, but only if I got a job, and I agreed.

The only reason they did this was because I had no way to get anywhere, but I knew that I really didn't deserve one.

However, later that week, I got a call from the moving company I had applied to; they had an open position and said it was mine if I wanted it. I happily accepted it for ten dollars an hour, working full-time. About a week after my job acceptance, my mother and father found me a 1996 Honda Accord for five thousand dollars. It had 88,000 miles on it, but was in good shape; it was perfect. I promised myself that I would change things now. Plus, I had Germany coming up in a couple months, and things seemed to be falling in place after my mom's birthday letter to me.

○ ○ ○

It was difficult to see all of my high school friends so happy during their senior year. *That could have been me*, I thought as I drove by in my tan Honda Accord and hooded sweatshirt. The first day I got my car, I picked up Rory, and it was like déjà vu. We rolled a blunt and picked up Tyler, who had these blue pills he called Vicodin. They were oval-shaped and he told me they were painkillers: I swallowed two whole pills and put another one under my tongue. After the blunt sank in and the painkillers weighed down my eyes, my ambitions decreased; I smiled and lit up a cigarette. This lifestyle was contagious. I tried to picture my mom's note, but the high was too peaceful.

I figured that I would celebrate for one more day before I started my new moving job. Jared came home from school after his first day in high school. It was crazy to think that he and I could have been in the same school together if I hadn't dropped out. In my heart, even though we didn't talk much, I just wanted him to graduate like I hadn't done. Jared would mention me that the teachers all wondered how I was doing, and didn't understand what had happened to me. They had said, "Your brother was such a wonderful athlete." I shrugged and walked away like I didn't care, even though it secretly felt like a knife through my damaged heart.

The next day I started my job and I woke up at six a.m. and put on my steel-toed work boots and drove to Wilmington, Massachusetts for work. I bought some Dunkin' Donuts coffee and smoked a couple of cigarettes before I arrived. Walking in, I wasn't sure what to expect until I saw a crowd of guys outside the trucks, all smoking cigarettes. There must have been twenty guys, all scruffy-looking with ripped jeans and hoodies. The supervisor came outside and read of a bunch of names.

"Tim, Stan, Greg, Jared, Jason, Logan. You're all going to Lynn to move out a middle school."

So part of our job was to move furniture for eight hours straight. We carpooled in Jason's car, all of us packed in together, as Jason lit up a cigarette and blasted his rock music. *These guys are bums*, I thought; even though I was a dropout, too, I felt out of place. I guess I still thought that I was something more than this.

In the car, Jared pulled out a joint and we all got stoned before getting to the job site. I stayed quiet, packed in Jason's claustrophobic car. We finally arrived and I was so high that I could barely lift anything. We all started to make our way into the school and started to move desks, chairs, file cabinets, and whatever else. *This is going to be my life now*, I thought. *This is the life of a high school dropout.*

The day was so boring and, by the end, my back felt like it was broken. The guys I was working with were all heavier and more muscular; I was a lean five-nine and one hundred sixty pounds.

I finally got home and my mother was at work again. I could smell the pot burning in Jared's room upstairs as I tossed my boots onto the floor and dropped on the couch. It was hard to imagine that my life would be moving furniture every day for forty hours a week. All I could think about all day was getting home, showering, and going over to Rory's to kick back and drink a forty-ounce.

When the first weekend came, I really needed to let loose.

Tyler and I got some alcohol, of course, and we started to get a nice buzz by taking shots of Grey Goose vodka. Tyler used to sell weed on the side, but had spent all of his money on alcohol. I had gotten my first check and decided to call a couple different people for cocaine. There was nothing like getting a nice drip down your throat and smoking a cigarette after.

"Fuck, who has yay?" Tyler said. We must have made a million different calls until, finally, Tyler's buddy, Sal, picked up. I leaned over Tyler's shoulders, looking like a puppy dog waiting for a treat.

"Just a gram," he said.

My eyes lit up, "Does he have any?"

"Yes," Tyler said in excitement. We jumped in my Honda, wasted, and drove over to Sal's house. His parents were home, so we walked in and went straight upstairs. Sal was known for selling pounds of weed, and he sometimes dabbled in cocaine. He pulled out a small white bag with a white rock in it. Most of it was solid, a little was broken up, with some powder. Tyler pulled out his debit card, poured a rock out, and started to chop it up as Sal rolled a blunt. I remember my knees shaking as Tyler chopped it up and I could smell the dollar bill against my knees.

SNIFF! "My turn," I said impatiently. *SNIFF!* Adrenaline took over my body as the drip numbed my throat and I felt immediate happiness. I was full of life, energized, and could talk about my deepest fears with the most intimacy. I could talk to a stranger about my life, as I ground my teeth and stared with wide, concerned eyes. We all had on our serious faces; we shared the look of being binged out of our minds. *I love cocaine*, I thought.

We walked downstairs and went into the backyard after doing another line. "Put a little on your cigarette," Tyler mumbled seriously. We smoked back-to-back cigarettes and then went back upstairs. Line after line, we finished the gram of coke at Sal's along with the whole bottle of Grey Goose; we were fucked up.

"Holy shit, it's three!" Tyler and I jumped in my car, feeling the anxiety of sunlight coming soon. I remember getting to my house, opening the door, and running to the fridge to get a gallon of water. I turned on the TV and flipped through the channels, grinding my teeth nonstop. I couldn't find anything to watch, my heart was beating out of my chest, and I thought I was going to die.

I just wanted to go to bed, but my heart was beating too fast. I thought that it could be my last night alive, and wished it would all just end.

I'm never doing cocaine again, I said in the back of my confused mind. My stomach was empty, but I couldn't eat a crumb. I tossed and turned for hours in bed, finally falling asleep as the sun rose for the day.

I woke up at three the next afternoon; my body was sore and I felt depressed. I went outdoors in my sweatpants to light up my last crushed Marlboro Red. My throat was dry and my lips were chapped as I lit it up. My mother's car pulled in the driveway followed by a grey Jeep.

My mother opened her door and so did the person in the car parked behind her. She walked up to me with a man who said, "Hey, I'm Rodney." He must have been around thirty-five, which was four years younger than my mother. I shook his hand hard although I was hung over, and introduced myself. After he left, she sat Jared and me down and told us.

"Rodney and I have been dating for a couple months now." I looked over to see Jared's eyes; they looked hurt. I ignored the news like it didn't faze me; the fact of the matter was that our parents had officially moved on and it felt like Jared and I had to choose sides.

Like always, Jared invited Vanessa over to take his mind off things; they had smoked weed in his room and had sex. My fourteen-year-old brother was having more sex than me.

Over the next couple of weeks, I continued to work, do cocaine on the weekends, and drink. Christmas was approaching and I hated it so much. I hated seeing my family, hated making small talk, and hated explaining how shitty my life was.

On my eighteenth Christmas, my aunt invited me to have our traditional celebration. I couldn't stand the thought of having to make up lies about how much I love my life. My mother begged me to visit, but I took off on Christmas Eve. I knew that it was so wrong to do, but I didn't want to face my family. Tyler was the same way; his mother had remarried, his father was an alcoholic, and his stepdad loved his own daughter and never made time for Tyler.

It was the night before Christmas, and Tyler and I got super fucking high. Not your typical Christmas story with bells and mistletoe; well, the mistletoe was the weed that we rolled into a massive blunt. While families were happily celebrating the one night a year when they could enjoy each other's company, eat sweets, and drink, Tyler and I sat alone in a piece-of-junk car in Sal's driveway. His family was away that night and Tyler and I had sneaked into a broken-down buggy in his driveway. It was freezing out as Tyler rolled up the biggest blunt I had ever smoked. The snow was falling, the neighborhood was decorated with lights, and you could see the neighbor's Christmas tree glistening in the window next door.

Tyler and I finished the blunt and noticed ourselves both dozing off while the snow fell so slowly on the ground. We looked in the window across the street, seeing the neighbors putting presents under the tree; the parents were dancing happily while the children were waiting for Santa. We came back to reality as we both turned to each other and laughed hysterically about how high we were. I think that secretly, though, Tyler and I both felt pain, and despised the feeling of being all alone. The holiday always made me sad.

On Christmas morning, Jared and I no longer ran to the Christmas tree in excitement, and instead we barely wanted to wake up. My mother would work on the holidays and Jared and I would only see my dad later on Christmas Day when he would stop by—things just weren't the same.

My New Year's resolution was to get up the courage to visit my sister. It was going to take a lot out of me, but she was still my blood. I was in denial about what was happening in my life. The football games at Hayers Stadium, where our high school football team would play, put my life into perspective. The year had started and, during the month of January, I must have experienced more drugs than I had ever had, and was plummeting down a rabbit hole; I was hooked. Tyler and I started to break apart from society and experiment with different drugs. We would talk with Rory and still hang out with him, but Tyler, a couple of Tyler's friends, and I had formed a drug group. This group consisted of kids who had also dropped out and who wanted to take their high to the next level. Here's how the plethora of drugs I took made me feel:

Marijuana: Paranoia, filled with uncontrollable laughter, and the munchies. Sometimes I'd feel like I had figured out the whole world with one single thought, and then *POOF*; it disappeared. Mood swings when I wasn't high by either bong rips, joints, blunts, or bowls.

Mushrooms: Tasted awful. They look like actual mushrooms except that they were skinny and smelled like shit. Made you feel out of touch with reality, otherwise known as "tripping"! I found myself hearing things that weren't really there and seeing blurred visions on the walls. Also, I was paranoid when coming down, followed by uncontrollable laughter. Sometimes, I felt out of sync with society, like a robot. Usually, I would consume these in handfuls.

Ecstasy: How could I forget ecstasy? It's exactly how it sounds. The first time I took it, I was so worried that I was going to die. Pills come in single, double, or triple stacks. They usually had symbols like dolphins, Mercedes, et cetera on them. You could swallow, snort, or chew them. I liked snorting them after the first couple of times because that way their effect usually kicked in quicker. You're filled with confidence, and life seems perfect; there is hugging and kissing, friends are the best, love is in the air. I'd never felt happier in my life. Walking felt like I was floating on clouds; sometimes I would rub my legs and the feeling was amazing. Side effects included severe depression the next morning, of course, because life is like a dream on ecstasy; I could talk to any girl with the highest confidence in myself.

OxyContin: Very expensive! It came in pills, twenty, forty, or eighty milligrams, eighty being the strongest. Usually used for back surgery or losing a limb: severe pain. My eyes would feel heavy, like a weight was sitting on them, along with the feeling of being so relaxed that your heart is barely beating. Eighty milligrams would make me doze off into unconsciousness as I smoked a cigarette burn into my shirt without knowing it.

Percocet's: Painkillers used for severe pain, similar to Oxy's. Very addicting; I usually couldn't move from the relaxation. I would be sitting on the couch, paralyzed by relaxation. Side effects can be tough, as this is a hard feeling to shake off.

Vicodin: Not as potent as Percocet. Usually came in the form of a pill, and could be crushed, swallowed, or snorted. I preferred snorting Percocet, but I wouldn't recommend snorting Vicodin as the pills can burn pretty badly. They were most often given as pain killers for wisdom tooth removal or minor surgery.

Klonopin: I loved those bad boys. They usually made me drift closer to the wall, as my body felt super relaxed. Lost control of my legs a couple times. I wouldn't recommend driving too often on them, even though Tyler and I did so all the time that year. These can be used for severe anxiety.

Submoxin: This was the strongest pill I'd ever taken. Usually used for ex-heroin addicts, along with methadone. That orange pill made me sleep for three days straight, and I woke up having no clue what had happened. I bumped into walls and had never felt so uncontrollable in my life. Not my favorite kind of scary, but maybe this was because I had mixed it with mushrooms and alcohol at the same time.

Heroin: The first time that I snorted heroin I was super-nervous. You hear all the stories of kids getting addicted. It's usually in a brown-like powder to snort. I would never put it in my arm. I snorted it in my car with Tyler. I didn't feel too much of its effect until I realized I had passed out behind my wheel multiple times. Not the best idea to drive downtown while snorting heroin. Fortunately, I only did it once.

Cocaine: Good old cocaine. My drug of choice when I was drinking. Sobered you right up. You can drink all night on cocaine. Laughter disappears, and is replaced with seriousness. Stories become deep and dark, teeth grind, there's drip in the back of your throat, sleepless nights, and, of course, it's never enough. I will get into this later, but cocaine is probably the most addictive drug that I had to stop.

Adderall/Ritalin: These were used for kids with a lack of attention span. Mainly, they were good for college students who couldn't focus. Not the best idea to sniff them. Similar to cocaine, but not as good. The drip is there; it's very addictive and never enough. Lack of sleep and fast heartbeats.

Free-Basing Cocaine: How could I forget sitting in my car with some aluminum foil and cocaine? Poured it into the aluminum foil and lit a flame under it until it melted and burned. Then, I'd slowly take a straw and inhale the smoke through my lungs. I guess you could say it's like smoking crack. Very addictive, but it didn't really do it for me.

I'm sure that I did a bunch of other pills, too, but honestly, I can't remember. Tyler and I would sniff anything, really, as long as it got us high. My drugs of choice, however, were cocaine, ecstasy, and alcohol. Scratch that, I didn't give a fuck what I did; anything was better than my reality.

The best part about doing all of these drugs was that the football games, basketball games, and any other event would become so much better. Before Tyler and I would leave for these events, we would get completely fucked up. Everyone who knew me gave me strange looks when they realized I was a burnout. I wore a hoodie over my head almost everywhere I went and smoked cigarettes left and right, lighting one with the other. Tyler and I, and a couple of others, would rob the team's locker rooms when everyone was watching the games. We did it for the high of avoiding getting caught.

◎ ◎ ◎

I went on a drug binge for a couple months, but then I needed to focus on not losing my job. I would try to only smoke weed and drink during the work week, especially because I had my trip to Germany coming up that my mother had already bought for my friend and me. My friend Tim had always been close to me; he wasn't really a jock or a burnout, just a regular guy. I was excited to travel across the world with him; I had never been out of the country. Just to think: it would be me, my old buddy Tim from basketball, Grant who was a popular burnout, and his girlfriend Lexy, all staying at a huge house in Germany—it was going to be a blast. We would be leaving in a couple of weeks and would be visiting there for two full weeks.

I took work off for those weeks, and honestly didn't care if I got fired; it was a shit moving company. I packed all of my stuff and counted down the days until I would be in Bonn, Germany. I also had never flown on a plane before, so it was pretty nerve-wracking. I had my friend Tim burn me a couple of CDs for the plane ride, mostly Tupac's music; he was one of my favorite rappers because I feel like we both had hard lives and, even though his was harder, I felt his pain of being raised by a single mother.

The fact that I was actually going to Germany made me feel kind of bad. My mother must have paid a fortune of her hard-earned money to send me there for my graduation present. What did *I* do? Oh yeah, I dropped out and started doing drugs; great kid. Anyway, the time came; I kissed my mother and brother, saying goodbye for two weeks. Tim and I sat in the terminal as I played my Tupac CD and waited to board the plane. My hands were sweaty as I entered the plane; it would be almost a ten-hour flight.

The takeoff scared me; I turned up the volume on my CD and could feel the beads of sweat accumulate on my forehead. My stomach got tight, and finally we drifted into the air. I closed my eyes and tried to fall asleep and forget everything. *I need this vacation from my awful life,* I thought as I closed my eyes.

"Welcome to Germany!" *Holy shit, we're here*, I thought as I immediately looked out the window. *Not much of a view*, I thought as I saw nothing but plain streets and trees.

"Logan, let's go!" Tim yelled. The four of us unloaded our bags from the plane and we walked outside—we were officially in Bonn. I lit up a cigarette and put on my forward-facing, tan Nike hat. The inhale was magical as my lungs filled up with smoke.

I heard, *"Hallo, hier drüben!"*

"What?"

Lexy knew more German than I did. She said, "Hello, over here. That is Monica; she is going to be taking us to David's house where you boys will stay and I am staying with her." I was kind of upset that Lexy wouldn't be staying with us; I had hoped that we would get drunk and that she would fuck my brains out.

We all packed into Monica's small car, which had a stick shift. As we packed in, I looked around and it almost felt like I was in another world. It was such a relief to see a different environment. The trains were everywhere, the streets were old stone roads with no lines, the houses had such different architecture, and even the air smelled different. We arrived at Monica's home and she brought us in to meet her parents. Lexy was going to stay with her, being the only girl, of course.

"*Hallo!*" Monica's parents smiled and hugged us. They loved Americans; this was amazing to me. All of us guys sat down on the couch and had a cold beer. I had no clue what kind of beer it was, but it was different from what we drank in the US. Her parents welcomed us and chatted as we laughed like young adolescents out of place. After getting a nice buzz on, Monica dropped us off at David's house.

"*Hallo!*" David's parents opened the door. David's dad looked exactly like Bob Saget from *Full House*, so Tim and I cracked up and tapped each other on the shoulder. We always knew what each other was thinking. Their house was a beautiful home with clear, glass walls and polished wooden floors; I had never seen anything like this in the US. It was so much more modern-looking. We walked in the kitchen to see David's mother; *I may have fallen in love today*, I thought. Tim's, Grant's, and my mouth all dropped to the floor.

She was an angel sent from heaven. She had on a tight purple t-shirt, which showed her big breasts and she had short, wavy brown hair with streaks of blonde and red. Her lips were covered with purple lipstick to match her sweater, and they were so voluptuous. Her thighs swayed sexily as she came over to us young boys; we all gasped for air. She wrapped her warm arms around us all, awarding us with huge hugs as she kissed us all on the cheeks. We all blushed as the room heated up and I thought, *I love Germany!*

We unpacked all of our stuff in the basement as David showed us the room. We threw our stuff on the bed and jumped on each other, screaming with joy and excitement; *I didn't deserve this*, I thought. We all called our parents to let them know the flight landed safely and told them that we would be careful.

The first night in Germany was amazing. It was a bit chilly out, so I put on my American attire. I threw on my dark jeans, white Nikes and my nice tan sweater with my fitted Nike hat. We definitely looked like Americans as we jumped into the German taxi. The driver knew right away and greeted us in English as we arrived in downtown Bonn.

My knees were shaking with anticipation as we entered this whole new world. For some reason, it felt like I belonged here and I wished that one day I could vanish here and never come back. Girls and guys partied in the streets, the stores were different, and there were sex and marijuana shops out in the open. The restrooms were open, with every sign leading to bars. It almost felt like heaven for us guys. We arrived at the bar called Studio 54 and we all got a table together. Grant ordered shots of Jägermeister for us all.

"Cheers to the best vacation ever! Again, Cheers! Cheers! *Charsrsr!*" We all got wasted; Grant fell off the barstool after trying to arm-wrestle some huge German guy. Most of the Germans were laid-back and could drink way more than us, even though I managed to keep up with them. What can I say? I was an American alcoholic.

"America, America, land of the free, mumble mumble," Grant sang, wasted; Tim and I carried him down the street. We threw him in the cab and then we all stumbled into David's house and walked in to see his mom standing there. She looked so fucking amazing, I never realized how badly I wanted an older woman until that day. If I had been coming home this drunk in America, my mother would have killed me, but in Germany, it was the exact opposite. She must have sat us at the table and gave us Fanta and three sauerkraut sausages each. They were amazing, and as she smiled while watching us eat; I became convinced I was in love.

Morning arrived, and my head felt like it had been smashed with a baseball bat the previous night. "Wake up!" David jumped up and handed us each a beer; it was only ten. *Germans drank like fish, but, screw it, I* was *in Germany,* I thought as I grabbed a beer. We all walked to the school that David's brother, Simon, attended; he was a year older than David. We walked down the streets, having a blast while drinking and smoking cigarettes. Simon's school was having a play in a couple hours. He said that we could drink while watching the play.

"Are you fucking serious?" Grant said. Germany just kept getting better and better. We all bought foreign beer at the liquor store and walked up to the school to watch *Annie* as we drank; this was going to be awesome. *No Beer Allowed,* the sign said.

"What the hell, Simon! You told us we could bring beer in?"

"You can," he replied. "Just sneak it in." We must have been five people away from the security guard as we stuffed five beers down our pants, one in my coat, and another in my pant leg.

"Next," the security guard said. We smiled and said, "*Hallo*" cockily as the guard waved us in. Immediately as I stepped into the school, a beer fell out of my coat pocket, spraying everywhere as we all darted into the hallway. Even in Germany we were causing trouble; we laughed and hid in the bathroom stall. After staying in there for a few minutes, we found our way into the school play. I'd never felt so cool in my life. As we walked in, the room drew to us, since it was clear that we were Americans due to my goatee and forward Nike hat. A smile in the crowd caught my eye and I realized that I couldn't stop staring.

Her skin was light, but tan, her eyes were baby-blue, and her hair was short and wavy blonde. *Her smile makes Katie's look crooked,* I thought as she grinned at me. I swallowed my tongue and fell in love on sight as she turned, blushing. I had to talk with this girl; what was the worst that could happen? I couldn't help but stare and as we looked into one another's eyes, I felt a connection—we had each found our soul mate. The play ended and the crowd scattered, but I kept my eyes on only her.

"Move," I said to people in the crowd. "Move, move." *Wait, there she is. Where is she going?* Gone; she had vanished. *I'll never see her again,* I thought, frustrated as I sipped my beer.

"Let's go, Logan," Lexy said as she grabbed my arm. I had forgotten about her, just like I had forgotten about my dream girl, Katie. There had been so many women that I had fallen in love with—so many women that I'd never had the courage to tell. *Another disappointment, Logan,* I thought as I walked away.

"We're going to some nightclubs tonight," David said. We went back to his house, showered, and got ready for the clubs; I had already been drunk far earlier than 4 p.m. We arrived at the club around six p.m., and the lights were raving and the girls were dancing sexily. The bouncer let us all in and the girls came up to us to dance and grind.

"I'm definitely moving to Germany one day," I told Tim as we took shots and grinded with sexy German girls. *Was I dreaming?*

In America, all of the girls I had ever known were stuck up and wouldn't dance with you unless you owned a BMW and made a six-figure income. In Germany, these girls just wanted to have fun! We all stepped out of the club at midnight to have a cigarette as we met a group of women.

"Are you Americans?" they asked, smiling. *Three beautiful blonde girls; this has to be a dream,* I thought as they all smiled with perfect white teeth and stared at us with blue eyes. We all flirted with them, until the fourth one walked over. My heart sank and, even though I was hammered, I got nervous and red.

"What's wrong, Logan?" Tim said.

I awkwardly replied, "Nothing; I'm good." Then, I remained silent.

It's her, I said under my breath.

"Hallo, I'm Eva," she said in the most adorable voice as my heart cried for her.

"*Auf Wiedersehen!*" they all said, which was goodbye in German. I shook my head in disappointment. My dream girl was right in front of me and I still couldn't even make a move. *I hate myself; I'm such a fucking wimp.* I got angry immediately, as I needed to go back into the club and get another drink.

"No, you're good," someone said as my chest was held back.

"What the hell?"

"You've had too much to drink."

"Fuck you," I said drunkenly, as I looked up to see the bouncer. He must have been three hundred pounds, and fierce. I said "fuck you" again. The thing about hard liquor was that I thought I was the Incredible Hulk every time I drank it. Tim grabbed me back right before I probably would have gotten rumbled into the ground. He dragged me outside as I cursed and yelled at the bouncer.

Of course, the night wasn't over, and we continued on to the next bar. We all stumbled into the bar as the bouncers stared, but somehow let us in. We took shot after shot, grinded with girls, and had a blast. Somehow, I again found myself outside smoking a cigarette, alone. The feeling was scary; it was the knowledge that you're so fucked up, and you have no clue where you are or how to get home. Now, I would feel like this almost every time I drank; however, this was an even scarier feeling, since I was thousands of miles away from home.

"Logan!" I turned as Tim found me. "Dude, you disappeared for like three hours; where the fuck have you been?" To this day, I still have no clue what had happened that night, but, apparently, I had disappeared and everyone had been looking everywhere for me. The night ended with a safe bed and a blackout at David's house.

We all pretty much slept through the day and chilled downstairs while David went out with his family. "David has a cat?" Grant asked.

Tim replied, "No, he doesn't have any pets."

"Then what the fuck is that cat doing in our room?" he asked and laughed hysterically. We all must have laughed for hours straight, realizing how drunk we had been last night. We had let a stray cat into the room. We pushed it outside using the pillows, and laughed some more.

"Last night was nuts," Grant said. "Logan, what happened to you?"

"No clue, man" I said as I cracked up. "Good times."

After resting for a day, we had Carnival to attend. Carnival was a German tradition where everyone would dress up in costumes and drink in the streets all day. I had needed the day of rest to prepare for this. We started at nine a.m. the next morning.

"Carnival!" David yelled as he woke us up wearing a costume that I almost couldn't look at. He wasn't wearing a shirt, but he didn't mind because he looked like a blond German male model with washboard abs. His bottoms consisted of a furry white skirt with disco boots. I know what you're thinking; I had been wondering the same thing. David wasn't as flamboyant as he dressed, however; he had a gorgeous girlfriend who didn't speak English—she would just stare at us, which we found funny.

We Americans, of course, wore normal clothes; I wasn't really into dressing up. We roamed the streets and started to drink beer. As we approached the city area of Bonn, the streets filled up with crowds, and the crowds turned into a parade. We marched drunk, singing some song I didn't know. We shouted and threw beers as we drank. For once, I forgot about my life back at home and felt at peace.

◎ ◎ ◎

A couple days before heading back to the States, we went out to the middle of Bonn. Downtown was packed, and the air smelled so different than in America—I loved it. Tim, Grant, Lexy, and I sat in a back booth, where we started to take shots. The feeling of drunkenness took over my body as my face turned red from the alcohol.

"Nemo!" Monica, Lexy's roommate, yelled.

"Nemo, like the fish," Tim and I laughed. Nemo was Monica's boyfriend, which shocked us all as we laughed. He must have been forty years old and she was eighteen, but then again, in Germany, no one cared. I mean, the legal drinking age was eighteen.

Nemo and Monica joined us to drink as we all got wasted, laughing and enjoying ourselves. Nemo spoke broken English and was kind of hard to understand. He invited Tim and me outside to smoke a joint. "Hell, yeah that's what I'm talking about," I said. The best thing about Germany was that we could smoke joints outside the bar, like a cigarette. We passed a joint around, laughing and smoking until it had vanished. Monica came out afterward and told us that she and Nemo were going home.

Tim and I laughed as we high-fived Nemo, shouting, "Nemo! You're the man!" The night was coming to an end, so Lexy called a taxi to pick up her and Grant.

"We will walk," Tim said.

"Fuck it," I said. "I don't want the night to end; I am higher than heaven."

Tim and I remembered the walk. It was so crazy to think that we were walking the streets at three in the morning, high and drunk in Germany. We jumped on the curbs, smoked cigarettes, and shouted German songs like two free souls. After about thirty minutes of walking, Tim and I found ourselves laughing nonstop. Now, this wasn't like normal laughter: we chuckled and hooted and laughed out loud for ten minutes straight. We had both walked three miles in Germany after smoking angel dust; we found out the next day that Nemo had laced his joint with PCP, and the reason why we had felt so invincible and couldn't stop laughing was because we had been on a hallucinogen. To this day, no marijuana could ever compare to Nemo's; it had been the funniest night of my life and I wouldn't take it back for anything.

Over the next couple of days, we got hammered in the streets of Germany. I was almost on a two-week drinking binge. The funniest part was that I didn't once try any German food. They had a McDonald's that Tim and I would go to almost every night. The first time we went was surreal because, of course, we went hammered.

"Es it Big Mac, und fry," said the person behind the counter as we both cracked up. The menu was a little different, but everyone in Germany seemed to speak English well anyway. The McDonald's there was way better: you could drink beer in there and smoke; it was like a fancy restaurant, unlike fast-food chains in America.

I called my mother on a couple of nights to check in, but didn't want to ruin my vacation. It was the usual negativity when I called home; I just tried to ignore all of the bad things happening there while I was living the good life abroad.

Long story short, Germany was a shit show. Tim, Grant, Lexy, and I would piss in the street, since we were drunk almost 24/7; I had almost fought a huge bouncer; Tim and I had smoked angel dust; and I had fallen in love again. The last day there was dismal, especially when David said goodbye and his parents had to drive us back to the airport. We shook David's father's hand

and David's mother kissed Tim on the cheek and hugged him. Then, she approached me to give me a tight hug, and she kissed me with her purple lips. Tim laughed as he saw my eyes light up; we both agreed that she was a very attractive older woman. We were all tired on the plane; I closed my eyes, thinking of Eva and hoping that someday love would find me back in Germany, and fate would put us together.

CHAPTER 10

NO FUTURE IN SIGHT

When we landed on American soil, I wanted to blow my head off—it was rainy and miserable. The air was different; it smelled like darkness and anxiety, but maybe that was just because I knew I was going back to a life I hated. I fell asleep after arriving home; I needed a good night's rest because I had work the next day at my awful moving company job.

"Fuck work, I quit. I don't need this lifestyle," I decided. So, there was another job I had disappeared from, and I had no clue how to pay the bills. My mother looked worried as I told her that I had quit, but I reassured her that I'd find another job quickly. The problem was that I had no clue what to do. I was a high school dropout, and it made me even more depressed knowing that all of my old friends would be graduating this year. I couldn't even imagine where I would be ten years from then, if I even made it, and I honestly was not sure if I even wanted to make it.

I spent that day smoking weed and driving around in my car. Even though I had been caught once and went to court, I didn't give a fuck—I had nothing to lose. I saw a moving company in Wakefield that was hiring, so I pulled over and put out the joint that I had smoked. I walked in, high as a kite, and filled out a job application. A lady came out and interviewed me, and I realized what a loser I had become. There I was, wearing a tan hoodie and beanie and reeking like weed. After a couple of questions, she hired me on the spot. *I must be in the twilight zone,* I thought. I looked around and saw who worked there and finally got a grip; I wasn't any better than these guys. Deep down in my heart, I knew that I had the potential, but my depression and drug use had taken over at some point; the world had stolen my heart and ambitions.

That was it, another moving company job for ten dollars an hour. This is really what my life had come to. I had gone to the ATM afterward to see if I had any money left at all, and found a big surprise that cheered me up. I had expected my bank account to say twenty bucks, but opened it to see three hundred and twenty dollars. At first, I thought it must have been a mistake. I canceled the transaction and put my card in again, expecting a new balance, but there it was again. "Hello, money!" I said as crisp twenties poured out. Since I hadn't accounted for this, it was like free money, I figured. I'm not sure what happened that day but I wish it hadn't, because it seemed to open a door for me that changed my life forever.

I would start my new shit job in a couple days. Until then, I figured I would get as high as possible and tell my mom I had a job, so she would be happy. Since I had some extra money (thank you, magic ATM), I called my drug dealer. Rory was sleeping, so I drove over to my dealer's by myself and went up to his attic. He had pounds of weed on his table and was also growing it in his closet. His parents were much older and had no clue what was going on.

"I'll take a half ounce," I told him, "Here's three hundred." Yeah, you guessed it right—I spent all of my money on marijuana.

"Why don't you just take an ounce?" he said.

"I don't have that money," I replied.

"You know a lot of people that smoke weed, right?"

"Yeah, I guess," I said.

"Here, take an ounce for free and sell it." *Keep my extra cash and smoke weed for free?*

"Fuck this three hundred dollars," I said, "Let's make some more." I mean, he had been selling weed for years and had thousands of dollars' worth of it for sale. "Let's do it!"

He tossed the ounce of weed to me and I knew as soon as I felt the nuggets in the bag that I was hooked in, and that my life was taking a turn for the worse. It felt so good to hold that entire ounce; maybe one day I would be able to hold even more. I took out a nugget and smoked it to my head as I drove home with an ounce of weed in my glove compartment. This was perfect; I could just tell my mother I was working, and instead smoke weed all day and sell it to my friends.

There I was, an eighteen-year-old, small-time drug dealer. *If only my father could see me now.* I felt like *the man* as I drove through our small town, in my tan Honda Civic that held an ounce of nugget; I passed the cops as they looked at me and didn't care. I told Rory that I was going to start dealing weed, and his friends began to call my cell phone and ask for twenty bags, eighths, and ounces. I sold the ounce in one day, made fifty bucks for myself, and had even smoked a whole bag myself. *This is awesome. By the end of the year, I should be making thousands*, I thought as my high mind raced.

I needed more weed, so I called my dealer. He smiled when I came over; we must have gotten so high that I felt like I was in outer space, so high that I could feel my body twitch and shake in slow motion, my hair growing by the second, and my throat closing up as my mouth went dry. After a beer fixed that, he gave me my two ounces and I was on my way.

Over the next week, everyone called me for weed; I was the cool local dealer who would smoke with you and drive anywhere to sell you weed. My prices were better than anyone's. Over the next couple of weeks, I bought a scale to weigh out my weed for the perfect amounts. My mother thought that I was working at the moving company, but the truth was that I was out selling weed, smoking weed, and making money.

My routine during that summer wasn't preparing for college or taking the SAT's, but instead it was to wake up whenever the fuck I wanted and check my cell. There would be ten or so missed calls, all regarding weed, of course; my friends had kind of vanished and all I cared about was making money to pay my bills. The crowds that I met were awesome; I'd go from the jocks to the burnouts, from the hippies to the psychos, from the stoner girls to the first-timers—everyone got high. The last time I had been this popular was when they used to call me Ice! *Did they love me, or was it just the weed? Did they fake-smile at me for a discounted bag?* Whatever the reason, I was never alone and everyone knew my name.

On the days when my brother and mother were home, I didn't talk to them. I would stuff the weed in my underwear and walk past them quickly; my mother knew I was up to something, but she wasn't sure what. Jared spent every minute with Vanessa.

When I wasn't out smoking weed, drinking, and popping pills, I was at home counting my money, over and over. Even though it wasn't all mine, I loved the smell. Sometimes I would take ounces of weed and sit in the bathroom, bagging them up individually and counting. I had been selling for almost a month now and could pay for my car loan, gas, car insurance, and could even smoke for free. I mean, why would I ever work again? *At this rate, I can make thousands a week.*

The summer was here, which made me angry because I should have graduated this year. Kids I had played sports with were going on to college and to better lives; their parents sent them to beautiful four-year schools, all paid for; they got new cars paid for by their parents, and their lives were amazing. Most of my old friends were in serious relationships while I was, well, a dropout with no education, ignoring my family and selling weed, and I still haven't even met the new half-sister I knew I had. *Fuck my life,* I thought as I slouched in my car and smoked a joint to my head.

One afternoon, I headed home after picking up a quarter pound from my dealer. I drove home slowly, as usual, looking out for the cops, knowing that I had already been on probation and that the cops wanted my life to be over. A middle-aged man was standing on my porch when I arrived home. He was talking to my mother as I pulled up, my arm hanging out the car window, wearing my gold watch and smoking a cigarette.

"Logan," my mother said when I got out of the car. "Remember Rodney? We've been dating for a couple months now." My heart dropped and filled with hate as my blood pressure rose rapidly.

"Hey, what's up," I said calmly, and walked in the house. I didn't want my mother to see the hate in my bloodshot eyes, so I went upstairs to bag up my weed and count my money.

With the summer being here, a lot of old faces from school would throw parties before they went off to college. I knew I had a drinking problem, but had never realized how people saw the real Logan Michaels until one of these parties. A girl, Ashley, was having a rager just across town, so Tyler, Rory, and I hopped in my Honda with some weed and liquor. We had the bottle open, drinking and smoking in the car like we always did on our way to a party. I wish I hadn't gone to this party because when we walked in, it seemed like my entire high school was there, including my old friends who I hadn't seen in forever.

I walked in, wasted, my hat turned sideways, and a cigarette hanging out of my mouth. Everyone smiled when they saw me and gave me love, but they knew I wasn't the same guy anymore.

The one thing that never changed about me was my sense of humor, though; I guess I had gotten it from my mother. She had been through a hard divorce, raising two kids despite her pain, and she could always smile no matter what the circumstances. I figured that if I lost my sense of humor, then I was *really* in trouble because that was all I had left in this world.

As I chatted with my old friends, they told me how great life was and *blah blah blah*; it made me fucking sick how fake people were these days. I realized that I was officially distant and hated that reality. I sipped my Hennessy out of the bottle and my hate grew stronger. I bumped into a couple of kids from high school and snapped. A fight broke out, and I felt my body strength triple as I threw down kids twice my size. Rory and Tyler had to hold me back as I cursed like crazy. We jumped in my car afterward and I burned out over the grass and into the middle of the street, wasted; if I had been pulled over, I would have been jerked out of the car and arrested.

Somehow, we made it back to Rory's house even after I had driven on the wrong side of the road for almost the whole way back. I thought of my mom's boyfriend and my hate grew stronger as I swallowed the last of the Hennessy and threw the glass bottle out into the road. Even Tyler and Rory knew that I was gone. *BANG!* "There goes Logan, blacked out again," I heard Tyler say as I passed out on the lawn.

"I'm an alcoholic," I said to myself, as I fell onto the grass. I knew I was, because even after a night like that, I wanted to do it again and again and again. I have plenty of stories about my drinking that I could tell you about forever, but after falling down a flight of stairs, waking up naked, fighting multiple people, waking up wearing tights, throwing up at parties, and driving drunk every night, it's all pretty much the same old story. What would really get my heart racing, though, was when the cops would follow me as I drove drunk. Some nights, I would pray to God that I would make it home as my eyes saw double. I can't count the number of times that I had passed out at the wheel and had scraped another car or a guardrail, or drove onto someone's front yard. I had no clue how I had even made it this far. I drank every day that summer and, by the time summer ended, I was up to a half a pound of weed a day.

⊙ ⊙ ⊙

My brother would be starting his sophmore year, and I felt awful because I was sure the teachers would judge him immediately when they learned he was my brother. And Rodney was always around the house, which irritated me; I mean, I would see him more than I saw my own father. He worked crappy dead-end jobs and always came around with a six-pack of Heineken beer. When my mother wasn't home, he would drink one with us. Most nights when I would come home, practically blacked out, he would be sitting on the couch and would listen to me talk about my dreams and ambitions. The one night I slipped up was when I told him about my little business venture.

"Rodney," I slurred. *Burp. Wake up, Logan!* I continued, "Rodney, want to make some real money?" Rodney looked seriously at me, waiting for me to reply. "Here's the plan, Rodney—"

"Rodney? Logan?" My mother yelled.

"I'll tell you another time," I said before I stumbled into my room and passed out. I could hear my mom and Rodney arguing all night as I slammed the pillow over my head. Jared was in his room with Vanessa, probably smoking and having sex. I had no clue what he did anymore besides probation work, smoking weed, and hanging with Vanessa. On top of that, I hadn't seen my father for a while. He wanted to see me, but had his own problems with his psycho girlfriend. She hadn't come near my mother lately, or at least my mother hadn't seen her; she probably was still stalking her and Mom didn't even know.

School started for Jared, my friends went off to college, and I was making money selling drugs to kids. My mom's boyfriend noticed my newfound wealth.

"That's a nice gold watch."

"Thanks," I replied, cocky.

"We never finished our conversation that night," he said. I instantly knew this meant trouble as I opened my ears to listen.

Rodney was a city guy. He had grown up in Lynn, Massachusetts, he'd had a tough life, and had been in and out of trouble.

"Logan, I know that you sell weed," he said. "It's obvious; I don't think your mother knows, but your brother mentioned he heard some kids telling him about it."

My stomach tightened as I realized that Jared knew I sold weed. I had tried to avoid this because, even though I was a shitty role model, I hadn't wanted to get him involved.

"If I got you a pound of weed, could you sell it?"

"Yeah, I could. Easy," I said.

"I'm gonna talk with my dealer and see if I can buy a pound; we can split the profit fifty-fifty," he said. I knew that I shouldn't have said yes, but my eyes could see the money and my greed took over.

"Sure, let's do it." I figured that if I could get half a pound of weed from my dealer and a pound from Rodney, I could make over a thousand a week in profit, and smoke for free every day. *Screw working for someone else. No one telling me what to do every day? This is the dream.*

Sometimes, when I looked in the mirror, I'd decide that life was easier when I'd forget who I was. The weed made me depressed when I was coming down from a high, and the problem was that I smoked excessively so that I'd never have to face myself sober.

I looked in the mirror one rainy day, and I swear I saw a man who wasn't me. This man was distant; he was shallow, selfish, and had low self-esteem. My heart hurt after I saw this man, because I knew this man had more potential than the life he was leading. This man deserved the girl of his dreams; he deserved a perfect family; and he deserved to be happy. *Who am I kidding? I'll never be happy*, I thought as I turned away from the mirror. I never wanted to look back at this man again.

CHAPTER 11

MY EYES BLEED GREED

My heart raced faster and faster as the cop drifted into the lane behind my Honda Accord. My eyes were bloodshot and the marijuana had me paranoid. I guess I had a reason to be paranoid, though—there was a pound of weed in my trunk. The thought that, at any moment, the cop could turn on his blue lights and bust me made my heart beat even faster.

Each second that passed felt like an hour, until I arrived at my mom's house and let out a deep sigh. Rodney was there when I walked in and he smiled at me while my mom looked relaxed, finally having gotten a day off from work. She had run out to get some food to cook for us that night. Once she left, Rodney had me come outside to his car. He popped open the trunk and tossed me a pound of weed. My eyes lit up as I felt the greed take over my body. I stuffed the bag of drugs in my pants and went upstairs.

As I passed Jared and Vanessa, I could tell that they knew I was up to no good, but we didn't speak. I think that Jared knew I sold marijuana, but he never said anything. My mom then arrived home to make a beautiful dinner: pork chops, corn, mashed potatoes, and warm sourdough bread. We all watched TV in the living room, and the smell of a home-cooked meal made me feel warm inside. My mother worked a lot, and she loved having the chance to cook a nice meal for her family. As we all sat to eat, I couldn't help but think of my father and the sister I had never met. I wondered what Dad was doing; *Is he eating alone?* Did he think about me at all? We were so close in distance, but it felt so far.

After dinner finished, I ran upstairs to my room and saw that my phone had over twenty text messages from kids looking for weed. I bagged up individual portions and hopped into my car to make some money. I knew this road had to end one day and that I couldn't do this forever, but the rush was amazing. I had met so many new faces, and I would feel like their savior as I handed them weed; they would smile and hand me the cash. That night alone, I sold a half-pound of weed and went back to my dealer's house to get another half-pound. We chilled, smoked, and drank together, laughing with our handfuls of cash.

I left the dealer's house at midnight, driving home drunk with another half-pound of weed. I swerved down the street and almost crashed into the neighbor's mailbox. Some nights as I drove home, I thought of simply closing my eyes for as long as I could and driving into a tree. I didn't want to live this life anymore; I needed a way out, and I knew that I couldn't sell weed forever. Sooner or later it would come to an end, either on my terms or the law's. *What the hell am I going to do?*

The more money I made and the more marijuana I sold, the deeper I got in the drug game. I had met my dealer's dealer who had visited one time while we were all smoking. He was shallow, grimy, and seemed to have no cares in the world. He must have come over with five pounds of weed and an eight-ball of cocaine.

We sniffed lines, drank, and smoked until my eyes were popped out of my head. He drove a brand-new Mercedes, had a faded, graying goatee, and always carried a gun.

That was the first time I had seen a gun up close, and it scared the shit out of me. I acted cool when he'd put it out on the table, but it made me think: *if I keep in this game, would this be my life?* I had gone from an all-star athlete with good grades and a great family to a faded, shady drug dealer. I was uncertain about who I had turned into, but the money was coming in so fast that I couldn't get out of this game.

⊙ ⊙ ⊙

By the end of that fall, I was inundated so deeply that it was to the point where I had forgotten about life. I hadn't talked to my family in weeks and was only focused on making more money. I had officially chosen the lifestyle of a drug dealer. I was selling pounds of marijuana, and the characters I met started to get shadier and shadier. I would meet people in alleys, back streets, and strange houses where I had never been before. It was nerve-wracking; but I had never had to deal with people trying to rob me. I was a regular guy in a world of tough guys.

The night had been beautiful, a warm seventy degrees in mid-autumn. Rory, Tyler, and I all went over to our dealer's house to drink, smoke, and blow lines of coke; the usual. I had left all of my drugs at home that day; I had wanted a night off from dealing, to just have a chance to chill with the boys. My dealer had recently picked up a five-pound shipment of marijuana. Of course, we rolled blunts and smoked one after the other until we were high out of our minds, on top of being drunk. Just when I felt relaxed from the alcohol and marijuana, it happened.

BANG! The door slammed open, and my eyes lit up and I looked at the front door. What I saw made me jump out of my seat, along with Rory and Tyler. Three men, their faces covered with masks, holding machetes ran into the house, screaming.

"Give us the fucking money and drugs!" they yelled like madmen. They punched my dealer until he was knocked out and took all of his drugs. I ran to my car and my heart raced as I could hear the footsteps coming closer behind me. I slammed the door and burned out of the driveway just as the masked robbers ran into the street after me. My legs shook as I just made it out alive. I was shaking as I lit up a cigarette. *Holy shit!*

Rory, Tyler, and I all had gotten away, and *thank God* I hadn't brought my drugs with me. It had almost seemed like a set-up, as if the masked men knew that my dealer had just picked up a delivery. About an hour after the incident, we all drove back by my dealer's house. We opened the door slowly to find that he was on the couch with his head down, bleeding. He was smoking a cigarette and having a drink, and he was furious.

"What the fuck am I going to do?" he yelled, as he smashed a hole in the wall. "Five pounds they stole, and thousands of dollars; fuck!"

We sat on the couch with him and didn't know what to say, until we heard: FREEZE!

The cops had busted into the house to find us all sitting on the couch. Luckily, we had no drugs on us and had already drunk all of the alcohol and blew through all of the cocaine. They had gotten a complaint from a neighbor that three masked men had run into the house with weapons. They noticed my dealer's bleeding head, and called an ambulance. They questioned us each individually, bringing us outside by the cop cars. We all gave the same answer: "Not sure why they tried to rob us."

We were all summoned to court, however, and the reason for the summons was unbelievable. One of the officers had found a pill bottle with the name scratched off that was filled with Klonopins, and, after searching the house, they also found a joint that my dealer hadn't even known was in the house. The worst part was that the cops now had us all on their radar and were watching us.

"Logan Michaels," the judge said. "You were a witness to a robbery; please tell us what happened."

"Your honor, three masked men broke in and beat my friend up. They tried to rob us for our wallets and then left. I was able to make it out before they got to me."

The judge got the same story from all of us, but he didn't buy it. All of my friends were on probation, so he told us that even though he didn't believe us, he had no actual evidence that we had been in the possession of drugs. He told us that if we were in here again, there would be serious consequences and even jail time, and that he would be watching us carefully meanwhile. If you ask me, we got off pretty easy; they never found the men who had committed the robbery, but I had a feeling that it had been someone very close to us all.

After this incident, I started to think about whether I was prepared for this lifestyle. It was a cutthroat business, Rory had said. He was right—you couldn't trust anyone anymore.

◎ ◎ ◎

My father's birthday was in a couple of days and I was nervous to see him; it had been months since I had even talked to him. Plus, I still wasn't ready to meet my half-sister.

Jared and I walked into my father's small apartment and saw him standing there with a smile. He was happy to see us; he seemed to have a better relationship with Jared, the little brother. It was funny because my father and I looked so alike, and everyone had always told us we were twins, but now we were so distant.

We gave him a birthday card as I grew even more anxious; it was strange to think that I could be nervous in front of my father. It made me sad to realize that my dad—the same guy who had played baseball with me until the sun went down, had built me my first basketball hoop, had cheered for me at my games, and had given me advice—could seem to be such a stranger. It broke my heart to think about this, and I wished that things could go back to normal and that we could just have a beer and laugh about life.

"Want to meet your sister?" he asked. Jared and I looked at each other uneasily and I could tell his heart was racing as fast as mine.

"Sure," we said. He opened the door to a room with pink walls and toys everywhere; she was in her crib. Jared and I both entered the room silently, but we were thinking the same thing. I remember hearing Jared talking to my mom one night, saying that he had always wanted a sister, but why did it have to happen in the worst way?

Afterwards, we both left my dad's that day as changed people. Jared and I didn't say much; we both pulled up to Mom's house in silence. I think that we both wanted to be alone for the night. We both headed to our bedrooms and shut our doors.

◎ ◎ ◎

Winter had come and gone, spring had been a blur, and summer was unfolding. My old friends had loved their freshman year at college. Most of my ex-friends' parents now hated me and thought I was a bad influence. These were the same parents who had once loved me for the athlete I was; it's funny how people can change so easily and can be so quick to judge you. I hated them, too. They didn't understand what was happening in my life, and I could try to explain it to them until I was blue in the face, but they still wouldn't listen.

My brother was in a deep relationship with Vanessa; they

would spend all day together every day, and she basically lived with us. My mother and Vanessa had become close friends; my mother was almost like a mother to Vanessa at times. She came from a rich upbringing, but it wasn't her blood family; she had been adopted when she was younger by a wealthy family in North Andover. Her family didn't really understand our family, and it seemed as if they still didn't like Jared. He was on probation, so they thought he was a bad influence on Vanessa. At times, I wanted to solve all of the problems in my family's life, but then I'd think, *one man can't change the world.* Maybe one day I could become rich and resolve all of my mistakes. Until then, though, I sparked weed and pushed everything under the rug; I was still only eighteen, after all.

One day, maybe I could become the man I was destined to be, but, until then, I'll take it one day at a time, I told myself.

In reality, I was a drug-dealing pothead and an alcoholic steeped in self-pity. I threw away a great life, a clean life, and was cascading ever deeper into being a criminal and leading my fifteen-year-old brother down the same destructive path.

The dealer guy with the faded goatee and grimy look ran into me on the street one day. He liked me, said I had always had potential, and gave me his cell number to call if I ever wanted to start selling more weed or cocaine. He told me that cocaine was where the "real money" was at, and I could see why—it was extremely addictive.

I held onto his number for a while, since I was not sure if I wanted to go down that route. He was no joke; his life was complete, and he was a drug dealer who would die for it. His name was Blake and he must have been twenty-five; he came from a couple of towns over, closer to the city. He had lived a hard life and rarely smiled. I wasn't sure if he hated the world more than I did, but it must have been pretty close.

"Do you have any weed?" It was a scenario I had tried to avoid and had been afraid would come one day: Jared had asked me for drugs. "I know you sell weed; everyone knows it. What, you think I didn't know?" I grabbed Jared to shake him, but realized that it wasn't his fault. *Who am I kidding?* Everyone knew I was a drug dealer. He told me that everyone in the high school said I had some of the best weed around. I told Jared that I wouldn't sell him any or give him any, and warned him to stay away from it. Who was I kidding, though? I was a hypocrite. It drove me nuts that my brother smoked weed and knew that I was dealing.

"How long has he known?" I muttered under my breath.

That night, I had probably made the worst mistake possible, and, of course, it had to do with me drinking my face off. It must have been two a.m. and I had barely made it home from drinking at Rory's house. I don't even remember driving home. Jared and Vanessa were up watching TV, and they laughed at me as I stumbled into the kitchen and rifled through the cabinets, throwing food in my mouth.

"Hey," I heard from around the corner.

"What's up?" I said to Jared.

"Do you have any weed?"

In my drunken state of mind, I said, "Follow me." My mother was sleeping, exhausted from working another double-shift. I brought Jared and Vanessa up to my room and opened my closet; under a stack of clothes was an odor of marijuana. "Since you know anyway; take a look," I said to them.

Jared's eyes lit up as I removed the dirty laundry to reveal a couple pounds of weed. I felt so cool as I grabbed a nugget out of one of the bags; Vanessa and he had never seen so much weed. It felt good to have Jared actually admiring me for the moment, even though I should have been ashamed of myself. I rolled up a joint as we all went to the back porch. It was the first time I had smoked with Jared; now we got stoned and laughed together hysterically. For that short time, I finally had my brother back—

the brother who used to follow me around at my baseball games, the brother who used to look up to his older brother Logan.

The next morning, Jared and I went back to our old ways. It's funny how much alcohol could change you. We both said "What's up?" to each other, and I could tell we both knew that we loved one another, but it was more of an unspoken bond. Jared had started to hang out with the wrong crowd, too, which angered me. I didn't want that for him. He would hang out at a house down the road where the mother smoked weed, her daughter smoked weed, and the daughter's boyfriend, who was older than me, was a real problem. He was known for fighting, for robbing people, and for carrying a gun at times. It scared me to know that Jared was hanging around this crowd.

I actually sold weed to the mother and smoked with her sometimes. They knew me and relied on me. Her daughter was around Jared's age and her boyfriend must have been close to twenty. He was a shady character; I could just tell, and I tried not to associate with him, but he liked me. He was known for hanging out with older punks who would rob people and beat them up afterward. I had sold him weed a couple of times, but had never smoked with him; he just wasn't to be trusted.

The smart thing for me to do would have been to stop selling him weed. What kind of twenty-year-old smokes with fifteen-year-old kids and dates a seventeen-year-old girl? His name was Luke, and he reminded me of the scum of the earth.

The fact that my brother hung out with him made me sick to my stomach. I tried to warn Jared about him, but Jared wouldn't listen. I can't really blame him, since I wasn't much of a role model either, but at least I would never rob or intentionally hurt anyone. Jared started to spend a lot of time smoking weed with Luke and a couple of other older kids. He was heading down a dangerous path, and every time I tried to tell him not to do what I was doing, he ignored me. He continued doing community service until he was eighteen, while going to school. Jared was such a smart kid, and he had always gotten good grades; I just hoped that he would graduate, instead of dropping out like I had done.

Vanessa's parents resented Jared, which I think led him to become more depressed and made him smoke more weed. I'm not sure what Jared felt about his life at this point; he had the same situation as I did, but his situation must have been harder: he had been only twelve when our parents split up, then he had met a sister he had never known about, and had witnessed his brother becoming a drug dealer.

I was sure that one day Jared would tell me his story and talk about how all of this had affected him. I was too caught up in my own stuff to ask him, but I imagined that he couldn't have been feeling good during this time. Jared had fallen for Vanessa at such a young age; I couldn't imagine how he must have felt, with her parents scrutinizing his every move. I hoped that someday I could hear his side of the story, so I could understand what was going through his mind. But until then, I could barely handle my own life.

◎　◎　◎

It was a regular night; I had just gotten home from the convenience store where I had gotten a pack of smokes. I had just picked up two pounds of weed, and left it in my secret hiding place. The night was relaxing, I was high, Jared was at Vanessa's, and my mom was again working a double-shift. I watched TV, made myself a calzone, and chilled. My high started to come down, so I went upstairs to grab myself a bowl to smoke in order to stay high for rest of the night. I walked up the stairs and things seemed different as I approached my room. I walked into my bedroom, noticing that the door was slightly open. *Hmm, strange, I usually close my door. Whatever; I must be too high,* I thought. I tossed aside the laundry to get to my weed and saw nothing. *Huh? It must be in the back.* I couldn't even remember where I had put it; I was so high all the time that my memory had faded. Another layer of laundry, and still nothing.

"What the fuck!" As I ripped my whole closet apart to find nothing, I realized that my two pounds of weed had been stolen! I'd never felt so many things at once: the feeling of betrayal, of anger, of being sick to my stomach, and of confusion. I didn't even know where to begin. How could this have happened? Was it a conspiracy against me? How was I going to tell my dealer, who had fronted me the two pounds, that I had been robbed? I *needed* to find it. My heart raced and my forehead dripped with sweat as I ran out to my car in a panic.

CHAPTER 12

FROZEN TEARDROPS

After several hours of constantly thinking about who had robbed me, I found myself feeling dead inside. I couldn't trust anyone anymore; it had to have been someone close to me. I walked back and forth in my room and couldn't stop pacing, realizing that I would have to tell my dealer I had lost two pounds. *What was he going to do?*

Finally, I dialed the phone, hoping he wouldn't pick up and just wanting to disappear instead, since it would have been so much easier.

"Hello?"

Fuck, I said in my head. My voice was shaky. "It's gone."

"What?" he replied.

"I was robbed for all of the weed!"

I must admit, he wasn't as angry as I thought he would be, and it may have been because we had become so close over the past months.

"Just think of everyone you sell to," he said. "Is there anyone you can think of who knew where you hid the drugs?" My mind raced with so many people; I figured that I had to start somewhere.

As I paced back and forth, my brother Jared walked in and I immediately grabbed him and started to scream at him. His eyes lit up with anger and confusion as I yelled, "Where the fuck is it? Where the fuck is it?" But Jared honestly had no clue what had happened, and then admitted something that made me realize this had been my own fault.

"I did tell a couple of friends that you had tons of weed when you showed me that night."

"Who did you fucking tell?" I replied, beet-red and furious. He revealed some names to me, and then Rory, Tyler, and I hopped in my car, ready for war. We drove over to each individual house and interrogated everyone that Jared had named. Some were kids I didn't even know; we slammed them against the wall and threatened to beat the shit out of them. Others, I could tell, had no clue what we were talking about, but I was freaking out as the clock ticked.

When my dealer got around to telling Blake, his supplier, I knew I was going to be in deep shit. Blake wasn't just a small-time dealer; he had connections that would have killed me. I must have chain-smoked all day until I just wanted to fall asleep and pretend this was all a dream. I wish I could have shut my eyes to wake up in seventh grade again as the all-star basketball player.

After a full day of stress and panic, I threw myself onto my bed, although my eyes were still wide open from the adrenaline. *Who had robbed me, how did they know, and how was I going to get out of this?*

"Logan," I heard Jared say, as I laid on my bed, stressed out. "I think I have an idea who took it." I jumped up as soon as I heard this, as my brother told me the story.

"While you were out yesterday, I had Tammy and her boyfriend over to smoke." My stomach tightened as I immediately knew it was those shady motherfuckers. Tammy was a burnout and her boyfriend was the guy who was known for robbing people and for carrying a gun everywhere he went.

"I told them how cool you were and that you always had tons of weed on you and that you had showed me. I'm sorry, I didn't mean for this to happen."

I asked Jared, "Do you think they did it?"

"Yeah, I do," he said. I took a deep breath and sighed; I really didn't want it to have been them. The main reason was that I didn't have a gun or any protection and, if I approached Tammy's boyfriend, he would probably shoot me. Then again, what choice did I have?

I sat in my car outside Tammy's house holding a baseball bat. I had no clue what I was going to do.

I called my dealer, who had Blake over to his house, and had told him about the situation. *Fuck*; my heart beat out of my chest as I heard Blake say, "He wants to talk to you."

"Do you know who took it?" the dealer asked.

"I'm outside of their house now and I am pretty sure I know who it is."

"Go get it back," he said and hung up. *Fuck, fuck, fuck; this is it, I'm going to get shot and die.* My life had come to this; I just wanted to get shot and end it already.

I grabbed my baseball bat and stepped out of my car. I ran up by the side of the back door and could feel the sweat on my back, dripping. I was in denial as I banged on the door with the baseball bat. No answer, so I banged again. Still no answer. I kicked the door open and entered, ready for battle as I turned left and then right. I approached the kitchen area and saw nothing; I then ran upstairs to the bedrooms and kicked the doors in. Throughout the house I searched every square inch, nervously waiting at any minute to be shot and die. Nothing happened, though, and I ran back out to my car and drove away in panic. I lit up a cigarette immediately as my heart raced faster and I hit the gas harder.

I called Blake back and told him what had happened.

"Okay, come by the house," he said and hung up. I thought about just disappearing and driving to another state for a while, but knew that if I did that, my life would be over. I arrived at Blake's house.

"I like you, Logan, so I am going to cut you a break and I don't normally do this; normally, I would beat the shit out of you, but I see potential in you . . . and by the way, I have some inside information on what happened," Blake said. "So you were right; it was Luke, Tammy's boyfriend. He called up one of the guys I sell to after he broke into your house and stole your entire supply. What a stupid fuck; don't worry, we are taking care of it, but here's the problem."

I swallowed my tongue and said, "What?"

"Last night, Luke tried to break into another house to rob them. Unlucky for him though, they had an alarm on the house and he was arrested by the cops with your entire weed supply on him. He was arrested with two pounds, a gun, and was caught breaking and entering. He will more than likely be in jail for three to five years, but we lost all of your weed and I'm down a couple thousand dollars, so I need a favor from you."

I couldn't believe that this was happening and that Luke had been caught; I was happy that he got what he deserved. But what I was getting myself into now?

"Let's take a ride, Logan."

Blake and I got into his new Mercedes and he put his gun in the glove compartment. It was official, I thought, *I'm fucked now*. We drove into West Roxbury, a city right outside of Boston, which was known for bad crime and drugs. We pulled up to a house that looked abandoned and Blake grabbed his gun and put in behind his back as we both walked in. The house was dark and the characters looked shady; I thought, *This is where I'm going to die.*

"You got it?" Blake said. He tossed money to his supplier as he was handed a couple of ounces of cocaine. "Here, hold this, Logan," he said as I grabbed the bag. We got back in his car and crushed up two massive lines of cocaine and we sniffed it.

"Holy shit," I said as the coke rocked my whole body and lifted me out of my seat. This wasn't like any coke I had done before.

"It's called rocket fuel," he said as he laughed.

After a drive back from the city, he dropped me off at my car and gave me an ounce of coke. He told me to try and sell it so I could repay him. I hesitated, but didn't really have an option at this point; who was I to say no to a guy with a Glock in his glove compartment? I took the coke and drove home very paranoid; coke versus weed was a whole different felony. I mean, if I got pulled over with an ounce of coke, I was fucked, completely and totally. I drove home slowly and cautiously and when I arrived, my mom was up waiting for me.

"I know you were robbed and have been selling weed," she said.

"I don't even fucking care anymore, Mom," I said as I ran back out of the house. She yelled after me, telling me not to come back if this was the life I chose. I burned out and drove over to Rory's.

I hated the man I had become, and I knew I was killing my mother, but I couldn't stop it. My mother had tears in her eyes so many times and it made me so sad to think of what I was doing to my family.

Rory wasn't home that night, so I decided to sleep in my car parked in his driveway. *What a fuckin' loser I was—a high school dropout, selling coke, recently robbed, and now homeless.* My nineteenth birthday was approaching and all I could think about was where I would be five years from now if I continued this lifestyle. I think we all know the answer to that question: dead.

The night was freezing while I slept in my car, and unfortunately, this wasn't the last time. Rory's mom no longer wanted me staying at his house because she knew that I was selling cocaine. So, over that month of October, I slept in my car almost three nights a week. I showered at Rory's house in the morning and got clothes at my mom's house when she and Jared were working or at school.

After getting the ounce from Blake, I sold it in two days, and had given him all of my profits, and we had squared up. Every time he and I got together, we would blow lines of coke all night. The following day would be the worst I had ever felt—I would have severe anxiety and the shakes all day, and the only way for me to stop them was to take a Percocet or Klonopin, something that would mellow me out. I don't think I was ever sober anymore. It seemed like if I wasn't blowing cocaine, smoking weed, or taking pills, I was either drunk or sleeping.

I started to do cocaine every chance I got. There were a couple of intense nights that I will never forget. One night, Blake and I were selling a couple grams of coke to people in the city. We waited outside in my car; Blake had his gun on him and we had crushed up two massive lines each on my car registration. We each blew one, and I then took my license and crushed up the second ones, and afterward put my license back in my pocket.

We waited for the call to come inside and got ready to sniff the last of the lines. But before we got a chance, we noticed blue lights flashing behind us; I mean, imagine seeing a '96 Honda Accord just sitting on the side of the street, looking sketchy. Blake immediately hid the bag of coke and put the crushed lines on the registration under the seat. The cop was at my window so quickly that we barely had time to do anything. He flashed his light on me as I looked into it and sobered up immediately.

"What are you boys doing sitting here?"

"Sorry officer, we are just trying to text our buddies who are having a couple friends over and I got lost."

"Okay, can I see your license?" he said. Thankfully, he hadn't asked for the registration, which had two lines of cocaine on it, right under my seat. I reached into my pocket for my license, which I had just used to crush cocaine. I literally prayed to God as I wiped it off with my fingers before I pulled it out.

Moment of truth, I thought. "Here you go, officer," I said as I closed my eyes, hoping there were no cocaine remnants.

"Okay, Logan, just move it along and find that party," he said and handed back my license. Unbelievably, there had not been a trace of cocaine on my license: somehow I had managed to wipe it all off with my fingers. Blake and I snorted the last of the coke, sold the ounces, and smoked a blunt on the ride home. Someone had been watching out for me—again.

I had yet another close call in November, right before my nineteenth birthday. Rory, Tyler, and I all had started to drink at Rory's house, since his mother wasn't there. I had a gram of coke left and could either sell it for a profit or just snort it, so we snorted it, of course. The problem was that Rory's mother unexpectedly came home and kicked us all out. It was freezing outside as we all got in my car with the alcohol and the cocaine and started snorting lines.

After we snorted one and smoked a blunt, I was super paranoid, especially because Blake and I had almost gotten busted a couple nights back. We'd been snorting lines in an abandoned parking lot and just finished our last one when an officer pulled up. So tonight, we left my car in a parking lot and walked a block over to an abandoned playground; it must have been around midnight. We crushed up two lines for each of us and passed the bottle of Captain Morgan's to each other. We each snorted one line of cocaine, smoked a cigarette, and bonded. About ten minutes later, we needed another line; cocaine was so addictive, but amazing. We then snorted the last one as we lit up another round of cigarettes. We lit up a blunt after that, and I could hear a crackling noise nearby, but I just figured I was just paranoid.

"Do you guys hear that?" I asked; we were all tweaked out of our fucking minds on cocaine.

"Hear what?"

"Someone seems like they're close to us?"

"Hey," I heard, and I turned around as a police officer grabbed my shoulder. "Fuck," I muttered as we tossed the bottle and the joint and started to run. As I turned, I saw the officer running after me; he was a couple of feet behind me, and I could hear myself breathing heavily, but I kept sprinting faster than ever.

"Stop! Stop!" He quickly ran after us, yelling that we were under arrest; we didn't stop. I felt like I was in a dream running from the cops—it was surreal.

Tyler and Rory broke away and, as I found myself looking back, the cop followed me. A part of me told myself to just stop there and end it, but then I decided that I wasn't going out like this. The cop chased me for another five minutes until we came to a seven-foot fence blocking the street where my car was parked. *Three, two, one . . . jump!* I cleared the fence, and it must have looked like a track star hopping a hurdle; I turned to see the cop holding his hands on the fence, a look of amazement on his face, and then I was gone, running to find my car a couple blocks over.

I found Rory and Tyler after a couple minutes of driving, and we all sped away from the area.

My throat was so dry that I thought I was going to die as I stuck my face into the snow and swallowed, just so I wouldn't choke to death. My heart raced as I prayed to God that, if I didn't die, I would make things right and never sell drugs again. Of course, the night ended with me passing out in my car, after drinking a ton of hard liquor just so I could sleep. Cocaine would make me able to drink so much that I'm surprised I hadn't died from alcohol poisoning. *What a wonderful week to lead up to my nineteenth birthday.*

I hadn't seen my mother for a couple of months. She texted me on my birthday, telling me how much she loved me and that she didn't care what I was doing; she just wanted to make sure I was safe. So I went home on the night of my nineteenth birthday and spent time with Jared and my mom.

My father stopped by to see his oldest son, the man who looked so much like him, the man who was struggling so hard to find happiness and to find himself. I could tell that he knew we had grown apart and that he was sad to see me like this, but we continued to sweep things under the rug; after all, we were the kind of men who didn't like discussing our problems. The night ended and I fell asleep in my bed like an innocent young man.

That night, I didn't feel like a drug dealer, nor like a man who had been sleeping in his car, nor like a man who had almost been arrested on several occasions, but instead I felt like a man who was loved.

◉　◉　◉

Over the next couple of days, I tried to spend time with my family, and avoided selling drugs or getting into trouble. I mean, I had been in so many situations by now that it seemed like a sign from God that I hadn't been caught. Sometimes, I felt like everything I was going through was going to be a test for something later in life, something greater than this world, something far more important, and that maybe God was testing how strong I was.

One day soon after my birthday, there was a banging on the door of our house; it was a woman dressed in all black. She looked very professional and asked if she could come in. My mother asked who she was, and invited her in without a thought.

"Why, of course. Please come in."

"Tiffany Surrenti from DSS," she replied as she walked through the door. DSS stood for Department of Social Services. My mother asked what she wanted with us as Jared and I walked over to listen.

"I have a complaint from a woman who knows you, saying that you are an unfit mother."

My blood boiled because, right then, I knew that my mother was being judged for my mistakes. I had a feeling that the woman who had complained was my father's ex-girlfriend.

I laughed in Tiffany's face. "You have no clue what you're talking about." I was so furious that I could barely control myself. "My mother works sixty hours a week, provides us with a roof over our heads, tries to spend every minute she has with us, and, at the end of her shift, will put a warm meal on the table."

The DSS woman said she understood, but needed to sit down to talk with us. We all sat at the table as she opened her manila folder.

"Okay, to start, I was told that your son Logan sells cocaine and was involved with the law on several occasions?" My heart almost stopped as my mother looked at me.

"What? I don't sell cocaine; I've tried it before," I said as my face turned flush. *How the hell did they know?*

"Also, I am told your youngest son Jared was involved in vandalism?" My mother was furious, and she defended us.

"These are good boys; they are just going through a hard time."

I saw my mother in a different light that day. I saw not only a woman who was my supporter, but also my friend who would never rat on me or never think less of me no matter who I was. She had never stopped believing in me, no matter how low I sank.

The passion in my mother's eyes was unbelievable; the DSS lady left apologizing and said that she was a great woman. I knew that it was my fault that DSS had been there, though; I wasn't a perfect son—I wasn't even close to it—but in my mom's eyes, I was still her innocent boy who was a victim of circumstances.

We all knew that it had been the woman my father had dated who wanted my mother gone, the same woman who had sent a fake cable guy to come hurt Mom. I was so sick of people trying to hurt my mother, even though I was hurting her more than any of them. Every day, my heart ached when I thought about what I was doing to her; I needed to stop this lifestyle. *I'm so much more than this.*

The holidays approached and I spent them shooting pool. Christmas Eve was typically Rory, Tyler and me playing pool with all of the people without families. The only difference between myself and them was that I actually had a family that loved me to death, but I couldn't face them. I was so ashamed of the man I was; it was easier not see them.

My mother had to make an excuse once again to the family, telling them I was sick. Jared showed up with Vanessa and, for the third year in a row, there was no Logan. I felt so bad that my mother had to cover for me again on Christmas—it broke my heart. I always tried to shower her with gifts to make up for never being there, but she didn't care about the gifts. She just wanted her son to be happy and, most importantly, be part of her life.

I tried to give my mother money every month to help her out with the rent; I didn't have a solid job, but I would give her the extra money I made from dealing drugs. It was hard for her to keep a roof over her sons' heads in a decent town, but she made sure she did whatever it took. I couldn't believe it was a new year, and I didn't even want to think where this year would take me.

Despite smoking pot and being with his girlfriend constantly, my brother was doing well in school and was on his way to graduate in couple of years. And most of my old friends were in college, having a blast. I would sometimes check their Facebook pages to see them having fun at college parties and going to places like Cancun or Aruba for spring break. Everyone looked so happy; I hated it. I would think, *It should have been me, until life took my spirit away and I gave in to the dark side.* I felt like I was in another world at times, and like I was forever trapped.

Chapter 13

RUNNING OUT
OF TIME

I realized as I looked deep into her eyes that my mother carried the world on her shoulders. She was hanging on by a thread some nights, and other nights she would have amazing strength. She worked very much like her own mother had; it was a vicious cycle we could not escape. The landlord was raising her rent and she could barely pay as it was. If I was truly a son, I would have stopped all of my bullshit to help her out, but I wasn't a real son—I was a pot-smoking, cocaine-snorting punk who didn't care about anyone but himself.

She told me that we had to start looking for apartments in another town. She tried to do everything she could to keep us in a nice town, but, as a single mother who had to compete with families that had two healthy incomes, she just couldn't.

After I was robbed and fell under Blake's wing, things just continued to go wrong for me. Blake would pick me up in his Mercedes as I threw my hoodie over my head and slouched back into his seat. It was almost mandatory that we smoke a blunt before our pick-ups. We would drive through the city as he would collect his money at different locations; some shady spots worried me, especially as I was always on edge.

"Logan, I got a tip on a guy who is picking up tons of Ecstasy pills," Blake said. "The plan is to wait 'till after he gets them, and then jump him and take them all." I knew instantly that Blake was planning on taking me with him, but I didn't care.

Blake, Rory, Tyler, a couple other local guys, and I all packed into cars while we waited for the deal to happen. The reason Blake decided to do this was because the kid picking up the Ecstasy pills was new to the area, and he was a wimp who shouldn't have been dealing Ecstasy in the first place. We parked outside of the house three cars deep, smoking weed and snorting cocaine until we saw the drop-off. And there he was—the kid pulled up in his beat-up pickup truck as we all turned our engines off and waited for him to get back into the pickup and drive down the street.

After he got in, we slowly followed him, knowing that he would probably make a stop to check if the drugs were all there. All three cars trailed him slowly, and we pulled behind him as he stopped. The plan was going exactly like Blake said it would go. Rory and Tyler sat in their car behind us, as it was their turn to stick with the plan. Rory walked up to the pickup and tapped on the glass as the kid slowly opened his window, looking paranoid.

"Hey, man, can you help me out?" Rory asked. "My car is having trouble starting and I need someone to check the engine, but I have no light and my cell phone is dead." Rory wasn't making sense at all, but the kid got out of his car.

My heart raced from the cocaine and adrenaline. I watched Blake fly out of the car, punch the poor kid in the head, and knock him out.

"Grab the fucking drugs!" he yelled as Rory grabbed a bag full of Ecstasy; there must have been fifty pills in there. We rifled through his car while he was passed out on the ground.

We all hurried back into our cars and drove off, and the rush was overwhelming as I looked at Blake; he was cool as a cucumber. I knew that this was the life he loved. We drove a couple of miles down the road to check out the Ecstasy.

I'd done Ecstasy many times before then, but this night I will never forget. We were all high on cocaine and marijuana as Blake took three pills of triple-stacked Ecstasy pills, and then I took three along with Rory and Tyler. That was the night I probably should have died. *What would my mother have thought of me?* was all I could think of. I didn't want to take the Ecstasy, but the peer pressure had gotten to me.

An hour had passed, I Started getting off while I was in the bathroom at Blake's house after taking a piss. I noticed myself leaning over the toilet, almost passing out. I zipped up my pants as I looked in the mirror, and felt the most amazing feeling of my entire life. Every ounce of fear or sadness had vanished; I no longer felt bad about the life I was living, my body felt like it was floating in mid-air, and my mind was at peace. I couldn't remember the last time that my mind felt so content and happy. I literally ran out of the bathroom and out Blake's back door onto his porch, jumping down an entire flight of stairs like I could fly.

I swear that for that couple of seconds when I was in mid-air, I felt like I was soaring in heaven. I had no guilt, no cares, no sadness. *Why couldn't I feel like this all the time?* We all sat on top of my car, bonding, hugging, smiling, and laughing until sunrise.

Maybe a part of me had died that night because if heaven was real, it would feel like that. The next day, I woke up at five in the afternoon. My whole body was shaking and ached. My thoughts were dark again, and I felt a big cloud hanging over just me. I swear that for the rest of the night, I lay in bed and realized that I had felt heaven and was now experiencing hell. *How can someone go from being so happy about life to being so depressed?* I must have been in bed for a whole day after that, and when my mom came in and tried to wake me, I brushed her off. The truth was, I really didn't want to wake up ever.

Unfortunately, the next day arrived and I was back to my normal, miserable self. I didn't spend all day in bed, but my life sucked anyway. Blake gave me a pound of weed to sell, along with a couple grams of cocaine. I went through my day as I usually did, picking up calls from losers and potheads and selling drugs, while my mother worked hard to find a new place for us to live. Blake had told me that he had a friend who was renting an apartment in Lowell and that there was going to be a party at his place that night. Apparently, the apartment was right behind the University of Massachusetts Lowell, and he was having tons of people over.

Blake and I arrived at the apartment that night with liquor, cocaine, weed, and Ecstasy; we had it all. We must have blown three lines before we even arrived, and we had been drinking during the whole ride there. We arrived at the party, where there were tons of hot girls dancing and people drinking and smoking weed. A couple of the bedroom doors were shut, and as Blake opened them up, we saw that people were blowing lines in there. There must have been over thirty people in a little apartment and people were also outside, hanging out in the streets, drinking, and smoking; basically the whole block was filled with people partying. There were different types of people, though, because we were directly in the center of the city of Lowell. There you had college students partying for the first time, junkies in the streets partying, and people having sex in cars and behind dumpsters. People were passing weed from left to right and some were even blowing cocaine off of girls' breasts.

Blake was pretty well known because people feared him; he was a pretty big drug dealer who had been known to fight anyone who fucked with him, and I was one of his boys. I crushed up lines for people and we all snorted one after the other until I found myself in a room with five people in a deep conversation. These were people I didn't know at all, and I found myself spilling my heart and my life to them. When I was high on cocaine, it actually felt like these complete strangers cared, but that was just the cocaine. We drank together until sunrise and I could barely sleep from all of the cocaine; I eventually passed out on the floor with no sheets or pillows.

Lowell must have officially been the lowest point of my life. The people that Blake and I partied with were all dropouts, junkies, and others with no goals or ambitions. When I wasn't selling drugs during the day, I found myself in Lowell, partying. I even started to notice that I was snorting coke in the daytime. I was so alienated from society that people must have thought I was a ghost when they saw me. I spend many nights in Lowell, but a lot I couldn't recall because I had been so wasted. The nights I did remember made me feel lucky just to be alive.

Lowell became a place for lost souls, people who wanted to forget about their shitty lives. Some nights, I would drive home from Lowell so wasted that, if I had gotten pulled over, my life would have been changed completely. One time, I left Lowell so wasted that I drove over a three-foot-high curb and almost smashed my whole car. Times got rough and on some nights I'd almost fall asleep at the wheel, just praying that I would get home to sleep in my bed.

Lowell was filled with fights all of the time, too. I wasn't a fighter and I didn't think that I was tough at all. There were many reasons behind the fighting, actually. People were on so much coke and were so drunk that they thought they were the toughest out there. Also, we had a pretty close group of people who we knew, and when people from other towns heard about this magical place in Lowell, they started to come party there.

A group of kids from a rival town came to Lowell to party. Of course, we all got along and were blowing coke and smoking weed and drinking until an argument started. We were all in a small bedroom in the apartment. Now, there may have been like ten of us, blowing cocaine and drinking. Of course, there is always one kid who is too hammered and gets in people's faces, being obnoxious. Most of the partiers ignored the obnoxious kid until he got in the face of Blake's friend. Wrong move; Blake's friend had anger problems.

"What's up, man?" he said as the kid got right in his face.

"Can you back up? Don't talk to me."

The kid immediately started to get defensive and got up closer to Blake's friend's face and start swearing at him. I was right next to Blake's friend and could see the anger in his eyes start to form as his fist began to clench.

"You got a problem with me being in your face?" *BOOM*! I swear to God, I had never seen anything so disgusting in my life. Blake's friend punched the kid in the face three times and the kid's eyes rolled back into his head and his teeth flew out of his mouth as he dragged against the wall, sliding down, unconscious.

Immediately, everyone stopped the music after hearing the disruption. Some kid I'd never seen before ran in; he must have been like six-foot-six and muscular.

"What the fuck did you do to my friend?" He grabbed Blake's buddy and knocked him out, and he had five more friends who ran into the room to beat on Blake's friend. All of a sudden, I was in the middle of this small room with a lot of people swinging fists and some people knocked out on the ground. Then, worst case scenario, the lights get turned off, and I found myself getting punched in the face. My adrenaline raced after I got hit, and I punched back as hard as I could, and heard my opponent falling to the ground.

Bottles were being smashed over people's heads and televisions were being thrown on people. The fights spread into the living room and throughout the whole house as the girls started to scream and run out. Then Blake was fighting some huge kid one-on-one and we all gathered around him, chanting and cheering.

"Smash his fucking head in, beat his ass, Blake; get him, Blakey!"

Blake knocked the kid out, and we all ran out the front door and jumped into our cars, bleeding, and drove away as fast as we could, before the cops came.

"Holy shit," I said to Blake as we burnt out, passing the cops who were heading to break up that party. I looked over at Blake and saw that his head was pretty fucked up, his eye was swollen shut, and he was dripping blood as he laughed. *This guy is fucked,* I thought.

Just another night in Lowell, I thought as I fell asleep. From there on, Lowell must have had a fight every time I was there. Kids from other towns would come by to start shit, and when there were fights in the street, the cops would come. I must have run from the cops dozens of times in Lowell; it was almost a regular thing.

If I wasn't running from the cops in Lowell or driving home hammered, I was sitting on stairwells in hallways, blowing coke with strangers or passing out face down on a sticky floor. It was becoming bad; my lowest nights took place there and the people I partied with weren't truly my friends—they were just there for the drugs, like me. I guess I had forgotten what a true friend was because for me, it definitely was almost never a person who was always there for you. I had people who were always there for me, but I always had to supply them with drugs to ensure their loyalty.

◎ ◎ ◎

My mother finally found a new place to live and told us that we would be moving in a couple of weeks. She had an old high school friend who owned a house in North Reading; he had a basement for occupancy downstairs. The area wasn't bad; it was a nice town, but our place would just be smaller and it was underneath his place. The rent was a lot cheaper and Jared could continue to go to North Andover High School until he graduated. He would be a little further from his friends, but the address wasn't too far from North Andover. We moved on a beautiful April morning into our new place. I was hung over, of course, and felt like death, but managed to help my mother move us into the new home.

Our place was a cozy, three-bedroom apartment with a small kitchen and old, rug-covered floors. I had my own small room, Jared and Vanessa shared a room, and my mother had the biggest room. It was pretty musty in the basement, but it was all we could afford. I tried to give my mom money for rent as often as possible, but I wasn't making a lot from selling weed anymore, mainly because I smoked away all of my profits.

On top of that, DSS stopped visiting, but I needed to figure out a way to persuade them I wasn't a drug dealer. The cops also knew my name and were starting to trail me whenever they saw me driving. I typically drove with at least a pound of weed in my car, and sometimes cocaine, too; if I had gotten pulled over, my poor mom would be officially perceived as a bad parent.

I started to look in the papers for jobs again; the problem was that no one would hire a high school dropout. After thorough searching, I found a construction laborer position for twelve dollars an hour, paid under the table. It was work for a builder who owned a realty company and was building new homes around towns like Andover, North Andover, and Boxford.

The interview happened in a trailer at the construction company. I walked in wearing my forward-facing black Adidas hat, like a punk. I was always very polite, though, when it came to speaking with adults. I chatted with the receptionist and then saw a man walk in who had been staring at me. He must have been in his early fifties, muscular, and well-groomed with pearly white teeth. He shook my hand hard and looked at me with a smile.

"Steve Sardou. How are you?" He offered me a position on the spot and wanted me to start in a month, working full-time when they started the new project. I didn't want to work full-time, but it was either this or back to the want ads, reading minimum-wage job listings again. I said yes and walked out, not knowing why I did it, but I think that in the back of my mind, I was slowly trying to start over and help my mother.

I arrived home, excited to tell my mom that I had gotten a new job, but of course she was not home; she was working late again. Jared and Vanessa were in the other room as I sat down and laid my head against my mother's old leather couch. I took a deep breath and thought to myself, *How am I going to get out of this hell of a life I'm living?* I had no girlfriend, and the nights that I'd been with a girl were clouded by the fact that I didn't know whether she loved me for me or if loved me for my marijuana and coke.

My phone rang later that night—it was Blake. "Logan, I need you to come to a pick-up with me." My eyes were tired and my lungs felt like they were on their last breath, but I had to go.

"Sure," I said. He picked me up in his Mercedes and passed me a blunt once I got in the car.

"We need to pick up some money from my connection in Roxbury." We drove into the city as my eyes drooped from the marijuana and my paranoia increased higher than a kite. "I'm going in to pick up the money; you watch the car and hold this." He put the gun on my lap as my heart raced and my sweaty hands held the gun. I really didn't want this lifestyle anymore; it wasn't me. I sat, the lookout guy, with a gun in my hand, and I could feel my eyelids lower as I denied that this was my life.

I looked down at the gun and thought about ending it all: no more pain or disappointing my mother. Minutes later, I realized that my hand was gripping the gun tightly as my arm lifted it closer to my head. As my arm raised higher, all I could see was a picture in my head: my mother's eyes staring at me. I heard whispers saying, "Logan, this isn't the life for you; I believe in you." My eyes almost teared up as I lowered the gun, and then I saw Blake come out of the house.

"You ready?"

I handed his gun back to him as I turned my face to the window, just hoping to arrive home to see my mother. I finally got home that night to find that my mother was sleeping in her room; as I saw her, looking like an angel, sleeping so peacefully, I mumbled under my breath, "I love you, and I'm sorry."

◉ ◉ ◉

My first day at the job was brutal. I had to work from eight-thirty to four-thirty. I woke up and smoked two cigarettes as I drank my French vanilla iced coffee from Dunkin' Donuts. My new boss, Steve, had just bought a property in my hometown of North Andover. The site was in the rich part of town where my old friends used to live; working there, I was just hoping they wouldn't see me. Steve mainly had me take trash out, carry wood, and help out other contractors on the site. He worked me hard, five days a week throughout the summer.

On the weekends and after work, I would sell pot and go to Lowell. I would still get into all sorts of trouble throughout the summer, but at least now I could give my mom a hundred dollars a week toward rent. I wasn't able to save any more money and was basically just working to live, getting high every day and blowing cocaine and drinking on the weekends.

Some nights when I got home from work, I thought, *Is this life? This is it?* My car was running like shit and had a hole in the muffler, which made it scream. I had to put thousands of dollars into it, just to maintain it. I was nineteen years old and living at my mother's house, watching the world pass by me. I was so stuck in my ways that I continued to deal weed and small amounts of cocaine to have some extra money, but I spent most of my profit. On the weekends, I could be found drunk and passed out on a floor somewhere in Lowell. Summer went by so quickly that I didn't even know who I was anymore until one day near the end of August. I clearly should have seen this night as another sign from above, but I was ignorant, as usual.

On an August Saturday morning, I went over to Blake's house to smoke a joint and to pick up my weed. He tossed a pound of weed to me to sell and also handed me a joint so I could get stoned on my way home. He also needed me to give one of his friends a ride home, which I had no problem doing. His friend lived downtown, so we lit up the joint and smoked it on the ride into the city of Lawrence. I swear the higher I got, the louder my exhaust sounded. I started to get paranoid as I drove into the city because my car was so loud, and I had a pound of weed tucked under the spare tire in my trunk.

We must have been five minutes away from his house in the middle of downtown Lawrence on Broadway Street. The city was busy and many eyes were on my car because my muffler was damaged; it seemed like the hole was getting bigger and louder. Out of nowhere, something led me to look in my rearview mirror; just a hunch, you could say. In the distance, I saw blue lights flashing as my stomach got tight and my heart froze with hope that the lights weren't for me. The cop passed one car, passed another, and was now two cars behind me. *Please God, don't be for me; it can't end like this.* His lights approached closer and the siren got louder. *Please God, make it not be me,* I thought, *make it be for the car behind me.*

My eyes closed as he passed the car behind me, and I pulled

over to the side of the busy downtown street, hoping he would continue past me. Nope.

"Do you know why I pulled you over?"

For some strange reason, when he pulled us over I didn't care; my heart wasn't racing and my nerves were calm. I think I had been through so much shit lately that I just wanted it to be over with. I was sick of running, sick of being a person that I never wanted to be.

"Yes, officer, because my car is loud; I'm trying to get it fixed."

He looked at me in disgust and had me step out of the car with Blake's friend to sit on the curb. I looked like a degenerate, wearing a baggy, plain white T-shirt, baggy shorts, and work boots that I had just thrown on to leave the house that morning. People were driving past us while we sat on the curb looking like burnouts, as the cop started to search the front of my car.

He searched the car because it smelled like weed since we had just smoked a massive joint. On top of that, I was ridiculously high with, now, two cop cars at the scene. Good thing we had thrown out the joint; however, he found a little piece of weed on the floor. "Is there any more marijuana in the car I should know about?"

"No, officer, there isn't," I replied.

"If I find any and you lied, you're going to jail. I'll tell you what, how about I ask your friend, and if he tells me, then only you will go to jail, or you can give me five hundred dollars right now, and I won't search your car."

The officer was smart, but not smart enough. He thought that I didn't know what he was doing. If I agreed to give him the money, he would know I had marijuana in the trunk. I honestly didn't even fucking care what this crooked cop was saying anymore.

"Go ahead, ask my friend if I have any."

I didn't even know this kid, but I was putting all of my cards on him. The cop pulled him aside and I saw them talking as I sat on the curb without care in the world. I wanted to go to jail; I was sick of my life, it was finally up, and my time was now. The guy came back with a smile and I was sure that Blake's friend had tattled on me.

"Your friend says there's nothing and that you were giving him a ride home. Still, I don't believe him; are you sure you have nothing in the trunk?" he asked again. "This is your last chance, Logan; either tell me and I let you off easy, or I find it and you go to jail."

For the split second, I saw an image of my mom crying, with me in jail, and all of my dreams to make things right vanished. I hoped one day to make things right again, but I had waited too long.

"Go ahead, officer, search my car." The officer looked shocked as he saw me look right in his eye and give permission.

Now, you might think he would believe me and not call my bluff, but he replied, "Okay, great; I'm going to pop the trunk then." He walked over and with each step he took, I swear I could see my life ending. He popped the trunk and, of course, saw nothing except a spare tire. Under the spare lay my fate. His hand slowly went to the spare tire as he smiled; the heat beat down on my forehead as my whole life flashed before my eyes.

BEEP! BEEP! "We have an urgent matter; there has been a shooting; we require assistance immediately." If I ever believed in signs from above, this was the time. The cop slammed my trunk shut and said, "Get out of here." My fucking mind was blown; was I the luckiest guy on earth here, or was someone looking out for me? Blake's friend and I jumped in my car and drove away, both silent the whole way back.

I had never felt so relaxed to just sit on my couch and watch TV. If things had gone the other way, I would have been calling my mother from jail, sitting in a cell, and awaiting a trial date.

That night, I had the whole house to myself; my mother was working and Jared was out. I smoked a joint to my head and laughed, watched T.V. and ordered pizza. *Thank you, God.*

◎ ◎ ◎

September arrived and my brother was now starting his school year, along with my former friends who were starting their sophomore year in college. It was another calendar year coming to an end, and I was stuck working at my dead-end construction job. I stopped selling pot for a month after the cop incident, but still went to Lowell and partied on most nights. All of my money went to my mom, though, and after I stopped selling for the month, money was tight. I was happy that I could give my mom four hundred dollars a month, but I had none left for me.

A few weeks later, Blake and I were at his house and he had a pound of weed just sitting on his table. "Toss me that; I'll sell it," I said.

He laughed and said, "I knew you couldn't resist."

I should have been in jail. I had basically been given a second, a third and a fourth chance. I knew it was just a matter of time before my luck would run out, but I didn't care.

Over the next couple of months, I continued to sell pounds of drugs, but was very cautious. I got my car fixed so that it wasn't loud, and started to make back that extra cash that I needed. My boss said I was a very hard worker and told me I was doing a great job. I think I always worked so hard because it took my mind off things currently going on in my life. Up until this moment, I had been so selfish that I didn't realize how much I was hurting my family. All I cared about was "Poor Logan" and ignored the fact was that it wasn't about me—it was about my mother. The night that transformed my life began with a phone call on Thanksgiving eve, right before my twentieth birthday.

Thanksgiving is a time for drinking, when all of the college kids come back to spend time with their families. Families reunite for another year, acting thankful and having a celebration. I decided to stay local, going to some bars in town, where I saw faces that I hadn't seen for years. My old friends were back from college and were excited to see me; they talked about how perfect college was and told me all of their bullshit stories about how successful they would be. I ignored it all and bought everyone shots, and then just continued to drink. My mother had the night off, so she was home with my brother, Jared. The locals and I all took shots celebrating another year, which honestly I didn't care about: I was just feeling lucky that I wasn't in jail.

I went outside to have a cigarette and to get away from all of the stories about college; I hated hearing them. My phone rang and I looked down to see that Jared was calling. Usually Jared wouldn't call me around eleven p.m. when I was out drinking at a bar, so I figured it must have been urgent. I picked up, but I was high and slurring my words.

"What's up?"

"Logan, I don't know what to do."

"About what?" I replied as I began to sober up.

"It's Mom; something's wrong with her," he said in a shaky voice.

"What is it?" I yelled.

"I don't know. Just get home; she's shaking and crying."

I had immediately gotten straight; I jumped into my car and drove home as fast as possible. I didn't even care about getting pulled over. *What's wrong with my mom?* I practically drove right up to the door and jumped out, leaving the keys in the ignition. I ran inside to see that my brother wasn't in the living room; I yelled his name.

"Jared! Mom?" Jared ran out, looking scared, looking like the very young man he was, and he told me to come into the room. When I opened the door to see my mother, it became a living, breathing nightmare. My heart raced with fear as my eyes slowly glanced up at her face. Her eyes had tears in them as she clenched her chest and wheezed. The look she had was exhaustion; she looked pale and empty of life.

I tried to hold my tears back as I ran over to her, as Jared anxiously called 911. I held my mother as she wheezed for breath, and I wiped her tears away. Jared screamed into the phone in the other room, "My mother's sick, she can't breathe and she's wheezing for air, please help!" After a minute of panic, Jared was able to give our address, and they were on their way.

Holding my mother gently in my arms, I could not disengage a feeling of selfishness. The feeling waved through my body into my chest, and I felt like I was going to lose grip of everything any minute now. I ground my teeth together as I tried to catch my breath and stay together for my mother. I held her as I gently helped her take deep breaths. "It's okay, Ma, deep breaths, I'm here for you." Her tears dried as she clenched my shoulder harder, and wheezed for air like it was her last breath. Each time she took a breath, I thought I was going to lose my mother. I wanted to cry so badly because I was not the son she wanted. I couldn't let her life end with her son being a junkie loser. I prayed until the ambulance came, which felt like eternity.

Jared opened the front door quickly and yelled, "She's in there!" The EMTs arrived and put an oxygen mask over her face as she gripped my shirt tightly, and she slipped into unconsciousness and was placed on the stretcher. Jared cried, and I called my aunt to come pick us up. My aunt arrived and rushed us to the Lawrence General Hospital. I felt so embarrassed. Drunk and high, I mumbled my words in the front seat of my aunt's car. All I could think about was my poor mother by herself, without me.

Finally at the hospital, I ran to the front desk and asked for

Maria Michaels. The nurse led me to her room, and as I entered I saw her. My face went blank; she was smiling. She was sitting up, her tears were dry, her face had some color back in it, and she looked full of life and super-relaxed.

She smiled as Jared and I hugged her, but we were very confused as she laughed. "I'm sorry boys, I suffered from the same panic attacks my father use to have. I hope you don't get them."

"Holy shit, Ma, you scared the hell out of us," I said as my chest relaxed and my worries started to fade.

The nurse then approached the room and tapped on the door gently. "May I come in, Maria? You might want your boys outside, I have some news you may want to keep private."

My mother replied, "These boys are my only reason for living, so whatever it is, you can tell me now. . . .

CHAPTER 14

THE END OF INNOCENCE

U sually our memories fade and we forget about things we have done in the past—or try to forget. For me, there was a crystal-clear moment on August 2. I still remember the smell of my dad's old car engine running as he worked under the hood. It was, of course, a Sunday, and he had the day off.

It was scorching hot, but with light humidity. The neighbors were out on their porch, an older couple who liked to sit and watch us kids have fun outside. We probably reminded them of how easy youth had once been. Our neighbors invited us to swim in their pool but for some reason we declined, maybe because we knew that just the four of us was all we needed that day. My father set up a sprinkler. Jared and I ran through the spraying water, laughing and pushing each other.

My mother had a patio set, with five-dollar plastic chairs and a foldable plastic table. It was tacky, and Jared and I loved it. She would bring us tuna fish sandwiches with Cape Cod chips and ice-cold glasses of water. She passed us our oversized towels that covered our whole bodies as we dried up under the sun.

After Jared and I finished our lunch, Mom would always tell us to wait about twenty minutes before we jumped up to go back to running through the sprinkler. We, of course, didn't listen.

"Boys, listen to your mother," my dad yelled at us on that August afternoon, exploding our fears. Jared froze up and I tried to not freeze as Dad angrily approached. I remember he threw down the rag he used to check the oil of his car, then shut off the engine and came over.

"Guys, you just ate; you're going to get a cramp."

Forlorn, Jared and I sat on the plastic patio furniture and waited as the sun scorched our faces.

After ten minutes or so, we both started to shut our eyes from the sun and doze, until we heard the back door open abruptly. My father stormed out in his bathing suit as he dove through the sprinkler like a little kid. Jared and I laughed as we jumped through again. Dad was, for a moment, a young kid. I still remember my father telling my mom, "Maria, let's go! You've been in the house."

She laughed as she sat down at the patio table drinking an ice-cold lemonade. She never jumped in but the look said it all. She had the family she always wanted, and even though we didn't have a huge house with a nice patio and huge pool, her heart was filled with love.

That memory of Mom's smile and joy had gotten me through that sad night at the hospital a week earlier. The woman now before me was beaten down and somber. She had suffered from years of panic attacks and depression, which we had learned to cope with. But, we were floored by the news of her physical condition: After doing some routine tests, doctors found a lump and diagnosed her with stage three breast cancer. She would start her treatment immediately and would have to put work on hold. Another devastating hardship for a woman who should have had a life of joy.

All I could think about, as I stood over her hospital bed, was that it was a warm summer day in August and I had my whole life and youth ahead of me. Now, at age twenty, I felt life's torment again and I realized that if I was to survive it—for myself and my mother—I had to change. It was time to grow up and live for somebody other than myself. My mother needed me; my brother needed me.

The doctors said that her cancer was spreading quickly, but there was a chance we could stop the spread. If not, my mom had just months to live.

Later in the week, I found myself researching breast cancer. My stomach clenched as I realized that the last impression my mother had of me was of a drug-addicted, unemployed loser—an underachiever, an embarrassment, a source of grief to her. *I'm a pathetic, selfish embarrassment,* I thought. *I deserve better. So does Mom. I am going to fix everything that I have done wrong in the past and show my mother and family that I can bounce back from all of this.*

My youth was over and I was ready to accept it. No more fucking around and feeling self-pity. I was going to be a family asset, not a liability. I would help put Jared on the right track, and prove to my mother that her older son was not a loser. Maybe in time I would feel whole again, like I did that Sunday afternoon so long ago, running through the sprinkler with my dad and brother.

A week later, after sleepless nights in the hospital, my mother was finally home. I would need to take care of her while she was out of work and adjusting to her new medication. My biggest fear was her cancer spreading to stage four, because the survival rate significantly decreased at that point. I was praying for all of this to just go away, but I'd had many miracles up to this point. Why would God do another for a selfish prick like me?

The first night home from the hospital was the first night Mom, Jared and I could finally relax. My mother seemed fine and upbeat. Maybe she was in denial about things, but I knew this wouldn't last forever. "What do you boys want for dinner?" she asked.

It blew my mind that she was still selfless enough to cook for us. I looked into her eyes and said, "No, Ma, it's time for me to take care of you."

She smiled and said, "That's okay, Logan. I love doing it." After about a minute of persuading her to let me cook she finally gave in. Maybe it was the meds, but she started to look sleepy.

I whipped together spaghetti and meatballs, just like my dad would do for me and Jared. I guess it was a simple recipe for a single guy. Once I'd served up a plate to both Jared and Mom, I looked at them and announced, "I'd like to say a little something."

"Dear Lord, I thank you for this food and another day of us being together. These years have been tough on us all, but out of tragedy there is always a silver lining. You have given me many chances over these years and now it's about time for me to make things right. Amen."

Jared and Mom smiled, but I could tell they didn't believe me. I couldn't blame them. I mean, had I ever really kept my word before now? Jared finished his dinner and said, "I'm going out with my friend."

I asked if he would stay until Mom fell asleep, but he refused. When I became angry he swore at me and stormed out the door. "Jared," I yelled as he took off. "Jared!" I yelled louder. "What a selfish prick," I said under my breath. I walked back into the house and saw my mother sinking lower in her chair. I covered her with a blanket and helped her to bed. As I shut the door halfway I glanced in at her. She looked so frail and cold. My eyes teared.

I entered my room and opened my bureau drawer to put away my belongings, and I saw my bag of weed; it carried enough for a joint. As Mom fell asleep I went into the bathroom and rolled up the last of it. Slowly walking outside I grabbed my lighter and sat on the porch alone. I scratched my head. I knew this was wrong, I promised my mom I would change. The agony flushed through my body in waves. It was as if I were trapped in a box, but there was no light, no escape, and no turning back.

I ground my teeth and became angry at myself and made my way to the bathroom. I shut the door as I breathed heavily and looked into the mirror. It was time. I jumped over the enormous emotional waves and broke out of the box and dumped my joint in the toilet and flushed it. "No more," I said. I looked into the mirror again, suddenly seeing a different person. He looked familiar; he looked like the ambitious self I had lost, and I knew what steps needed to be taken. It would be a long journey, but I knew what needed to be done.

The following morning I jumped into my car. The day was beautiful as I drove over to my father's house. I knew he had the day off, so hopefully I would catch him home.

He opened the door, looking as surprised as I was to see me smiling. He smiled back and I could tell we were both glad to see each other. "I need your help, Dad," I said. "Mom has stage three breast cancer and Jared is going down the wrong path. Please help me."

He paled and bit his nails. He sat down and put his hands over his head. "When did you find out? How bad is it? What can I do?"

We hugged, and I finally had my father back. It made me want to cry thinking that this man who had been my best friend and father had been out of my life for years. I had missed so many memories with him. As we hugged tighter he told me he loved me and missed me and that he was sorry for everything. "I'm sorry too, Dad. I never meant to distance you from my life. I'm back now and have to make up for lost time."

My sister came out of the other room looking tiny and shy. I picked her up and hugged her and smiled. "I'm your brother,

Logan," I said. My father smiled with joy and she looked at me, confused, but she had a little smirk on her face.

My dad said, "Logan, whatever you need, you let me know. I'm here for your mother. Let her know that, and I'm here for Jared."

I told Dad about my plan of redemption and that I was no longer going to be selfish and how I was going to make things right. My first plan was to get my GED and then enroll in community college. Over these past years I had let my depression and self-pity destroy the bright future I once had. I would have to work twice as hard as a normal kid, I would need to fix my mistakes, but I wasn't turning back.

After one month of studying for my GED exam, I was ready. I had not smoked weed for over a month. My mind was free and clear. Even though the first two weeks I felt like dying, I didn't give in. I continued to spend time with my mother. Her medicine was finally helping and she wanted to get back to work. She had a checkup with the doctor in another month. Blake, Rory, and Tyler had been blowing up my phone. I just ignored them. I didn't care about them. My family was more important and I just focused on cramming for the GED.

Finally, the day arrived when I would enter the doors to take my GED exam at Northern Essex Community College in Haverhill, Massachusetts. The entire ride there my heart was pounding out of my chest. I didn't eat anything all morning and felt sick to my stomach. My throat was dry when I finally arrived in the parking lot. I closed my eyes and took several deep breaths. I grabbed my pencils and threw them in my old JanSport high school bag that I'd hardly ever used and walked into those big silver doors.

The testing room was packed with all types of people—mothers who'd dropped out, kids who'd dropped out, people like me who all looked like they wanted to get their lives back on track. The teacher asked me for my ID and I passed it over to her. "Please take a seat. The exam will begin in ten minutes, you will have two hours to complete it."

My heart rate increased and everything in my body started to feel like jelly, as if I weren't real. Faces seemed to be glancing over at me, but I couldn't see them clearly. I started sweating. Each second felt like a minute as my body became hotter. Sweat started to pour off my face, and I felt like my world was slowly ending. Every glance my way felt like someone judging me. I took my shirt and wiped my face.

When I was nearly about to cry, the wave of unbearable anxiety suddenly passed. It was as if I was in control. I could smell the air again. My body cooled down. The teacher said, "Five minutes until we begin."

My heart rate relaxed and slowed.

I finished the exam in an hour. It concerned me that I was that quick, but maybe I was smarter than I thought.

When I got back in the car I saw a couple text messages from Jared. "Hey, Logan. Meet me at the hospital. Mom has her checkup."

I arrived into my mother's room after she was relaxed on the medicine. I told her about my test and that I thought I had passed and that things were going to get better. She smiled and looked proud but super tired.

Jared's eyes were bloodshot; he was texting someone. The scariest part wasn't that he was high but that he reminded me of myself when I started to lose hope in life, and more importantly, of myself. My mind began to race and the feeling of panic returned. I tried to ignore it, but it grew stronger. I ran to the hospital bathroom and slammed the door behind me. I soaked my face under the faucet as the man in the mirror became blurry. I broke into a sweat again and felt the tears well. I took several deep breaths until it passed. I wiped my face off with a towel and looked up in the mirror and found myself screaming.

As I looked in the mirror, I knew this wasn't going to be the last time this happened.

It almost felt as if I had the devil on my back, trying to self-destruct again. *Not this time,* I thought. I banished the demons who plagued me. Seeing my mother under that warm hospital blanket strengthened my resolve. I wouldn't stop at anything to redeem myself for her. I would continue to battle my demons, as they were sure to attack again and again. But this time it wasn't all about me. This time it was for my mother and my brother. I would be selfless.

ACKNOWLEDGMENTS

I wish to especially thank my mother who was not only my inspiration, but also my best friend. My brother Nick, whom I gratefully acknowledge: you inspired me to be a better man and to become a role model. And thanks to my father and my sister, Madeline. Also my nephew, Brayden, who brought me peace at times when I was sad. Just holding you in my arms helped me get through another day. I would also like to thank everybody who was involved in my life. I don't hold grudges. I have grown and become a better person. Much appreciated.

CPSIA information can be obtained
at www.ICGtesting.com
Printed in the USA
FSHW02n0817140918
52185FS